MW01136464

KILLING DREAMS

A SAM MASON K-9 DOG MYSTERY BOOK 5

L. A. DOBBS

This is a work of fiction.

None of it is real. All names, places, and events are products of the author's imagination. Any resemblance to real names, places, or events are purely coincidental, and should not be construed as being real.

KILLING DREAMS

Copyright © 2018

Leighann Dobbs Publishing

http://www.ladobbs.com

All Rights Reserved.

No part of this work may be used or reproduced in any manner, except as allowable under "fair use," without the express written permission of the author.

INTRODUCTION

Thanks for your interest in the Sam Mason Mystery Series! This series is set in small-town northern New Hampshire where anything can happen and playing by the rules doesn't necessarily mean that justice will be served. It features a small town police force and their trusty K-9 Lucy.

This is an on-going series with a completely solved mystery in each book and a lot of ongoing mysteries in the background. Don't forget to signup for my email list for advance notice on new release discounts:

https://ladobbsreaders.gr8.com

SUMMARY

"This novel combines the intense drama of a thriller with the gentle, down-home touches of a cozy. I'm eager for the next installment." Virge B., Proofreader, Red Adept Editing

A grim discovery in the woods of a small northern New Hampshire town uncovers a disturbing truth that might finally be what Chief of Police Sam Mason needs to put elusive drug dealer Lucas Thorne away for good.

But for Sam's second in command, Jody Harris, the discovery dredges up disturbing secrets from the past. Secrets that could damage her friendship with Sam.

Thorne is one step ahead of them until a surprising ally comes through with one final piece of evidence that will solve an old mystery and nail Thorne. Is the evidence too good to be true? Sam doesn't dare question it and kill his dreams of ridding the town of Thorne.

Meanwhile, Lucy the K9 has her own battle to fight as it seems the unwanted feline guest at the police station may become a permanent fixture.

CHAPTER ONE

Sam Mason's phone pinged for the third time as he pulled the White Rock Police Department Tahoe into the dirt driveway that led to the ramshackle farmhouse where Frank Buckner had lived for most of his eighty-five years.

He glanced down at the phone display as he slowed at the beginning of the long driveway, a knot forming between his shoulder blades as he read the texts. Two were from Harry Woolston, who wanted to stop by the station. The third was from his dispatcher, Reese Hordon, informing him that the brother of one of his officers was coming to drop off some things he'd found that might belong to the police.

At least Reese had used the phone instead of that dispatch system she'd talked him into installing in the car. Sam glanced down at the mic hanging under the dash. Most police departments had used these for years, but in a town as small as White Rock a computerized dispatch system was hardly necessary. Still, Reese had somehow gotten funding for one, and she claimed it would be easier and more efficient because he could answer while driving instead of having to pull his phone out. Sam hated the thing. All it did was squawk static. Plus, it was a change from their normal routine, and Sam was finding that the older he got, the less he liked change.

Sam coasted to a stop and picked up the phone to reply to both. Harry Woolston had once been chief of police of their small northern New Hampshire town, the same position Sam now held. Though Harry's tenure had ended decades ago, that didn't stop him from popping into the station and trying to insinuate himself into Sam's cases.

Sam understood that Harry was bored with retirement and wanted to reminisce about his glory days. That part Sam didn't mind, but Harry's insistence at getting involved was getting out of hand. In fact, one could argue that Harry's involvement and not listening to Sam's orders was what had caused officer Kevin Deckard's near-fatal shooting.

Harry was in a bad place right now. He blamed

himself for the shooting that had resulted in Kevin's coma. Unfortunately, that meant Harry felt compelled to come to the station even more often in an attempt to assuage his guilt. Sam knew he should tell Harry to stay away, but he didn't have the heart.

It had been two weeks since the incident, and Kevin's prognosis was uncertain. The doctors said time would tell. Kevin's brother had flown in from California, and Sam wanted to make sure they gave that the importance it was due. Kevin was a good cop, and he wanted his family to have some peace while they were hoping for him to recover.

So many things to do already and it was only ten past eight in the morning. Sam should have passed this quirky call off to a junior officer, but Frank Buckner had been a friend of his grandfather's and he felt duty-bound to take care of this personally—even if Frank's claim of his dog finding a dinosaur bone was a bit preposterous.

A whine from the back seat caught his attention, and Sam turned to see his German shepherd mix police K9, Lucy, lying down, her chin on her paws as if she felt the same way Sam did.

"I know, girl, it's crazy right?"

Lucy's brows lifted over golden-brown eyes as if in agreement.

"We'll just go see what Frank has. Let him down easy." Sam took his foot off the brake and drove the rest of the way down the driveway.

The late summer nights were starting to get cooler, but the mornings were still glorious, with sunshine warming the air and sparkling off the dew on the grass. Birds flew between tree branches, and squirrels were busy gathering acorns to store for winter.

Frank sat in a wooden rocking chair on his porch, wearing a blue flannel shirt. Steam rose from a mug cupped in his weathered hands. Sam's heart squeezed with a pang of loneliness for his grandfather. They'd been close, and Gramps had been gone only a few years. He missed him still. All the more reason to treat Frank with personal attention and respect.

Frank's face cracked into a welcome smile as he recognized the Tahoe. He put the mug down and slowly rose from the chair. Sam could practically hear his bones creaking.

They met halfway between the car and the porch and shook hands. Frank's grip was as strong as a 25-year-old's. His blue eyes danced with excitement.

"It's the darnedest thing, Sam. I never seen nothing like it." Frank ran a hand through his thick white hair. "I think it might be from some kind of dinosaur. Maybe it will even get in the museum."

"Maybe." Sam hated to dash the old guy's hopes, but he didn't want to encourage him either. As far as he knew, no dinosaur bones had been found this far north. Most likely it was a bone from a moose.

Frank's knees popped as he crouched down to pet Lucy. "Nothing like that's been found up here before, right?"

"I don't recall any dinosaur bones being found here, but let's not get too excited until we figure out what it really is." Sam looked over Frank's shoulder toward the porch. "So where is it?"

Frank stood, some of his excitement fading. "Well now, that's the thing. I haven't been able to get it away from Ranger. He must realize it's a rare find and doesn't want to part with it." Frank jerked his head toward the side of the house. "He's out back guarding it like it's a brick of gold."

Lucy glanced toward the side of the house and whined, then looked up at Sam.

"So, you haven't really seen all of this bone yet?" Sam asked.

"Well, not the whole thing, but it's got a big knobby end." Frank held his hands about a foot apart, then moved them a little closer, his expression now uncertain. "At least it seems big. I mean, it's bigger than the bones Ranger usually finds. Looks long, too.

Much bigger than the meat bones I get from the butcher."

Sam nodded. "Okay, let's go take a look."

Frank led the way to the backyard, Lucy trotting at his heels and glancing up at Sam to make sure he followed. As they rounded the corner of the house, Sam scanned the yard. He spotted Ranger, Frank's oversized Rottweiler, lying next to the back steps, the unmistakable ivory color of a bone cradled in his paws. Most of the bone was hidden because his chin rested on it. The hairs on the back of Sam's neck tingled. It didn't look like a dinosaur bone, but it didn't look like a moose bone, either.

Lucy stopped a few feet from Ranger, her ears straight up, her gaze riveted on the other dog. Ranger looked at Lucy warily. His lip curled, and he let out a low growl. Lucy looked at Sam, and Sam shook his head. No sense in getting into a dogfight over a bone.

Frank sidled over to Ranger, who glanced up at him with an apologetic look, as if he knew he was doing something wrong but wasn't about to give up the bone. "You're a good boy, Ranger. Now show your treasure to the nice policeman here."

Ranger's eyes flicked to Sam, and he nuzzled the bone deeper under his chest.

Lucy moved closer, getting between Sam and the dog and earning another growl from Ranger.

Frank cast Sam a sheepish look. "I'm sorry, Sam. He's usually very obedient." More knee popping as Frank squatted next to his dog. "Come on, buddy, we want to get a look at this bone. Could make us famous, you know."

Ranger looked as if he was considering his options. Frank extended his hand, and the Rottweiler eyed it dubiously.

Frank pushed further. "Come on, boy, you know you can trust me."

Ranger sighed, cast Lucy a suspicious look, and then turned loving, trustful eyes on Frank as he lifted his head off the bone.

"Good boy." Frank scratched Ranger's chest, then reached in and pulled the bone from between his paws.

He stood holding the bone out to Sam. "See, what did I tell you? That ain't no deer bone. Too big and not shaped right." His gaze narrowed with uncertainty. "It's a lot smaller than I thought it was. Maybe a small dinosaur? What do you think, Sam? Maybe there're some tar pits up there or something. We should look for the rest of the bones."

Sam stared at the bone. Frank was right about one

thing; it wasn't an animal bone. Frank was probably too invested in his earlier hopes that he'd made a rare discovery to realize the bone was a femur. From a *human*. And Frank was right about another thing, too. The rest of the bones were out there somewhere, and now Sam had the unenviable task of not only finding them but also figuring out who they'd belonged to and how they'd ended up here.

CHAPTER TWO

"I've already checked all the files. A hiker was reported missing a few years back up on Dixon Notch." Wyatt Davis rattled off the details of the missing hiker as he followed Sam through the old-fashioned lobby of the police station into his office.

Sam had called back to the station as soon as he'd gotten back in the Tahoe with news of the bone, and his small team had sprung into action. Wyatt was fairly new to the department, but Sam liked the way he took initiative. He was going to be a good addition to the team and much needed, especially because they were down one officer with Kevin still in the hospital.

Sam put the bone, which he'd wrapped in a towel, on his desk. He'd have to call John Dudley, the county medical examiner, and have him take it to the morgue. But right now he had a search to organize.

Wyatt eyed the towel. "The hiker was reported missing two years ago. How long do you think that bone has been out there?"

"Hard to tell. If animals got at it, they would have picked it clean and left the bone to the elements..." Sam let his voice trail off at the gruesome thought. He'd seen some chew marks on the bone. There'd been no meat left on the bone, and he wasn't exactly an expert on dating old bones.

Lucy, who had lingered at the reception desk to score a treat from Reese, padded in and scanned the office warily. Probably looking for the stray cat that had shown up at the back door a few weeks ago. Sam suspected the cat had belonged to their latest offender, a cold-blooded murderer who had been killed when he'd pulled a gun on them during his arrest. If the cat was his, then it was now homeless, and Sam didn't have the heart to kick it out even though the cat and Lucy seemed to be at odds.

"Don't worry, she's not in here," Wyatt assured Lucy.

Lucy cast one look at the towel on Sam's desk, then flopped down in a patch of sunlight beneath the tall arched windows that overlooked Main Street.

Stately oaks and maples lined Main Street, and the morning sun beamed through their thick leaves, causing dapples of sunlight to dance on the sidewalks. People strolled the street where the shops were just starting to open. Kids tossed a Frisbee on the grass in the commons. Just like any other day in a peaceful New England town, people went about their business not knowing that the remains of a body long lost lay hidden in the woods. Somewhere a family was waiting for this person to come home. It was Sam's job to do that, a job he took very seriously.

"Any runaways or other missing persons in the area?" Sam asked.

"I only searched a few years back and in this county. I'll expand the search. Would help if we could narrow down a timeline."

"Hopefully John can help with that. In the meantime we need to get out there and start searching. I can call in the Staties. Maybe Bev Hatch has some people she can lend, but I don't want to wait. Where's Jo?" Sam glanced back through the door into the bullpen of the police station for his second in command, Jody Harris.

"She went up to Nettie Deardorff's. Apparently Bitsy ate her petunias."

Sam smiled. There had been an ongoing feud

between Nettie Deardorff and Rita Hoelscher. Most of the complaints came from Nettie, who claimed Rita's goat, Bitsy, was damaging her property. Recently Nettie had adopted a chicken, and Sam thought it was mostly to get back at Rita. The two elderly women had been feuding as far back as Sam could remember, and he suspected their differences went much deeper than the goat.

Even though their calls usually amounted to nothing, it was important in a small town like White Rock to go out and smooth things over. He wondered how long Jo would be out there. Jo was his most trusted officer, and the two had forged a bond that went beyond working together as cops. Jo knew Sam's secrets. He knew she had his back. And he had hers, though sometimes he wondered if she was as forthcoming with her secrets as he had been with his. But today they had an important search to conduct, and while he wanted Jo's input on organizing it, he wasn't going to wait.

"She can join us later. I want to get out to the woods as soon as possible. Frank said he'd take Ranger out. Thinks the dog can lead us to the spot." Sam opened the paneled oak door to the small closet in his office.

The police station occupied the old post office and hadn't been updated since the 1930s. Not that Sam minded. He much preferred the honey-golden oak doors and scarred wide pine flooring to the newer building's indoor-outdoor carpet, beige walls, and steel desks. This place had character from the floor-to-ceiling windows with their intricately carved moldings to the antique brass post office boxes with their beveled glass panels and eagle motif that now served as a divider between the reception area and the squad room.

He grabbed a lime-green police vest and tossed it to Wyatt, then pulled one out for himself.

"Harry's on his way here." Sam turned to see Reese standing in the doorway. Her brows were raised over wide blue eyes as if questioning whether or not she should let Harry in. "And Kevin's brother will be here in thirty minutes."

Damn! Sam had been so focused on the bone recovery he'd forgotten all about Harry and Kevin's brother. He didn't want to put Kevin's brother off. He knew how important it was for the family members to get answers when an officer had been shot in the line of duty. But the responsibility of finding the rest of the bones and discovering the identity of the person weighed on him. He'd have to leave word for Jo to meet with Kevin's brother. Jo had worked closely with Kevin and knew him as well as Sam.

"Thanks. I want to get on this search as quickly as possible. When Jo comes back can you have her wait for Kevin's brother and then join us at the search site as soon as she's done?"

"No problem."

Sam bent down and grabbed a pair of hiking boots from the closet, speaking over his shoulder to Reese. "And tell Harry that..."

"Tell Harry what?" Harry Woolston appeared in the doorway beside Reese, looking at them curiously with intelligent blue eyes. He was thin and spry, his white cotton puff of hair contrasting with Reese's jet black locks as the two of them stood side by side. "Is something going on?"

Sam sat in his chair, toed his black shoes off, and started tugging the boots on. "Sorry, Harry. Frank Buckner found some bones out in the woods behind his place."

"Human bones?"

"Yep. We're going to find the rest of them."

"Oh, I see." Harry scratched his chin. "Old Bucky, huh? You sure you can trust what he says? He can be a little fanciful."

"Went out there and took a look myself." Sam gestured to the lump under the towel, and Harry's eyes widened.

"Ahh, that seems important. I just came by to see if you wouldn't mind a late lunch with Marnie Wilson."

"I think I'll be kind of busy today, Harry."

"Yeah, yeah. I see that. But you know Marnie really wants to help out and wants to get your take on a few things." Marnie Wilson was Harry's favorite candidate for mayor. Sam didn't really know her well, but Harry had been pushing hard for his approval. Not that he had to push that hard; the current mayor was no prize and pretty much anyone would be better.

"Maybe some other time."

"Yeah, see, her schedule is real busy and it would be a big personal favor. She has an opening later this afternoon and..."

Sam was barely listening as he laced his boot and mentally went over the list of things he'd need for the search. Orange vest for Lucy. Bug spray. Evidence bags and gloves. Flashlight. Lucy's leash... now where was that?

Sam pulled his bottom desk drawer open. Not in there. He opened the one above. He hardly ever used Lucy's leash because she was trained to stay by his side, but he wanted it just in case they ran into anything she shouldn't get into out in the woods.

"It would mean a lot to me, I'd consider it a big personal favor, but if you're busy..."

Sam's heart hitched at the dejection in Harry's voice. Even though Harry could be a pain, the truth was he had helped in several investigations. Sam didn't want to hurt his feelings, but the search was a priority.

"I don't know how long I'll be searching," Sam said. The leash was in the middle desk drawer. He pulled it out and looked toward Lucy. Wyatt had found her vest and was putting it on her.

"Good. Then you might still be able to go. I mean, if you find what you're looking for. I'm sure she won't mind if you're busy. I'll let her know what's going on and she can swing by. If you're here, good; if not, no big deal."

"Okay, fine." Sam was pretty sure he wouldn't be there. If Marnie Wilson wanted to waste her time swinging by an empty police station, that wasn't his problem.

"Good." Harry turned to leave. "Good luck out there. I'd offer to help but..."

"Don't worry. We have Lucy. She'll find what we're looking for."

Lucy's ears perked up as if she'd understood his words.

"Then I'll see you later." Harry left.

Sam pulled his flashlight from the drawer, stood and shrugged into his vest. "Reese, can you call Bev

Hatch and find out if she can join us? I'll let her know the location when we get there."

"Will do." Reese turned and headed back to her desk.

Sam looked at Wyatt. "Ready?"

"Yep."

"We'll take the Tahoe." Sam had a supply of gloves and evidence bags in the vehicle.

Lucy trotted to the door and waited for them.

Out in the bullpen, the cat sat on top of a filing cabinet, its paws tucked underneath, jet black fluffy hair puffed out all around it. It stared at them with ominous green eyes. Lucy gave the cabinet a wide berth, but that didn't stop the cat from hissing.

As they jumped in the Tahoe and drove back toward Frank's, Sam couldn't shake the feeling that what he was about to find in the woods would not be what he expected.

CHAPTER THREE

Sergeant Jody Harris eyed the white bakery bag on Reese's desk in the station's reception area. She could really go for a jelly doughnut right now, but the snug fit of the belt around her normally slim hips gave her pause. Maybe she should lay off the sweets for a while. She was pushing forty now and couldn't pack them away like she used to.

"Sam and Wyatt took off to search the woods to find the rest of the bones." Reese barely looked up from her typing.

Jo tore her eyes from the bag and frowned at Reese. "Bones?"

Jo had just returned to the station after a grueling hour of trying to settle the latest argument between Rita and Nettie. She'd finally gotten them to shake hands when Rita promised to buy a new flat of petunias and plant them. When she'd left, Rita was breaking out the fruitcake, and they were sitting down to tea.

She hadn't heard anything about any bones. What was Reese talking about?

Reese stopped typing, leaned her elbows on the desk, and looked at Jo. "Yeah, if you turned on your police radio you might have heard about it."

Oh, that. Jo wasn't used to having a dispatch radio installed in the Crown Vic—one of two official police cars the town owned. She kept forgetting to turn it on.

"Anyway," Reese sighed and pushed the bag of doughnuts toward Jo. "Turns out Frank Buckner's dog dug up a bone in the woods. A human bone."

Something in the back of Jo's mind stood at attention; her frown deepened. "A human bone?"

"Yep. A femur. You just missed them. They took Lucy to try to locate more bones." Reese nudged the white bag closer and Jo shook her head. Reese lifted her brow and shrugged before pulling a chocolate cruller from the bag. "He's going to text me the coordinates so you can join them. Bev Hatch is on her way. She mentioned something about notifying the state police."

Jo's mind reeled. Human bones in the woods were

bad enough, but Jo had a personal reason to be concerned — the *real* reason she'd come to White Rock in the first place.

Images of her kid sister, Tammy, flashed in her head. She didn't have many, because her sister had been abducted when she was eight years old. Jo had been ten, but memories of that time cut deep.

Her family had been torn apart by the subsequent futile search for the person who had taken her. The police assumed it was a serial killer. They'd captured someone who they *thought* had done it, but they'd never recovered any trace of her sister, and he'd never admitted to taking Tammy. Jo had been haunted by not knowing.

That haunting was what had sent her into law enforcement and what had eventually brought her to White Rock. After decades of investigating privately, she'd been led to this area when she'd gotten a tip that trees with certain markings—signs she suspected were connected to Tammy's killer—had been found in this area. She'd never found those trees, though, other than in a few grainy photographs connected to another case and whose locations were unidentifiable. After five years here, she'd finally decided to let go of the investigation, put it away, and move on with her life.

And now this? Could this be what she'd been

looking for the whole time?

"Earth to Jo..." Reese was staring at her. She tipped the open bakery bag in her direction. "You spaced out. I think you need a doughnut to keep your blood sugar up."

Jo peered in. No jelly? Darn it. She picked a honey-dipped doughnut and absently tore off a small bite. Of course Reese would have no idea why she was acting so weird. She'd never told anyone about her sister, not even Sam. That could present a big problem now if this bone was connected.

Jo stuffed another bite in her mouth and talked around it. "Any idea how old the person was or how long the bone had been there?"

Reese shrugged and munched the cruller. "John just came and got it. Said it's probably an adult and has been out there maybe a few years. He'll have to examine it closer. Wyatt thinks it might be a hiker who got lost two years ago."

The tension in Jo's shoulders eased. She glanced out the window toward the rolling blue mountains in the distance. That could be it. Simply a hiker who got lost. This northern town near the border of Canada with its unspoiled forests, pristine lakes, and ranges of mountains was a mecca for hikers. But the forests could turn unfriendly in an instant. Hikers got lost, and once you were in deep, those lacking the proper equipment could find it nearly impossible to get out.

"What did Sam say? Does he think the bone is that old?"

Jo swallowed, the doughnut tasting like sawdust at the thought of Sam. He'd become more than just a partner over the years. They had built up a bond. Sam had shared his secrets with her; why hadn't she shared hers with him?

She'd wanted to, but it seemed there had never been the right time. She felt guilty that her whole reason for hiring on here had been to further her personal investigation into her sister's disappearance. At first that hadn't mattered, but that was before she had gotten to know her squad mates.

The longer she'd worked here, the more the place had grown on her. And Sam, too. Their friendship meant a lot to her, and she didn't want to risk it for anything. Even though they were *just* friends, she couldn't bear the thought of not working with him every day. Sam would be hurt if he knew she'd been holding back on her sister's case. She needed to tell him soon, even if this bone wasn't related.

Jo shoved the rest of the doughnut in her mouth and brushed the crumbs from her hands. "I need to get out there."

"Not right now. If you'd had your radio on, you'd know that you have to meet with Kevin's brother in ten minutes."

"Kevin's brother is coming here?" She really needed to get in the habit of turning on that radio.

"Yeah. He wants to talk about what happened and drop off a few things. Some thumb drive and Kevin's badge."

Darn! Jo couldn't put it off, especially because Kevin had taken the bullet meant for Lucy. The bones would have to wait.

"Sam will let me know the coordinates and you can join them when you are done." Reese went back to her typing.

"Okay, thanks."

Jo headed to the coffee machine and grabbed a K-cup and her yellow smiley face mug. At least this would give her a chance to load up on caffeine. She'd need it if she was going to help search for bones in the woods.

With the mug full, she headed toward her desk when...

Hiss!

Something sharp snagged the collar of her shirt.

"Ouch!" She turned to find the fluffy black cat

sitting atop the filing cabinet, looking at her with faux innocence in its alien-like green eyes.

"Cut that out!" The filing cabinet was as tall as Jo, so the cat was positioned above her, staring down with a look of superiority. "You know, I'm beginning to regret fighting to keep you here at the station instead of taking you to the animal shelter."

The cat's eyes narrowed slightly.

"Is Major bothering you?" Reese appeared at her side, a noxious smelling nugget in her hand.

Jo turned to Reese. "Major?"

"Yeah. Major Payne. Major for short. That's what I'm calling him."

"Him?"

Reese nodded and held the treat out to the cat, making soft cooing and clucking noises. Major regarded her with suspicion.

"Yeah, it's a him. Eric gave him a wellness check and all his shots. He needs to be neutered, by the way." Eric, Reese's boyfriend, was going to veterinary school.

Major's paw shot out, slapping the treat from Reese's hand.

"Guess he doesn't like the idea of being neutered." Reese picked the treat up and plopped it on the filing cabinet in front of the cat. He simply glared at it.

"Lucy might get a kick out of it, though." Jo took

her coffee to her desk and left Major glaring at the treat.

The cat had shown up at the back door a few weeks ago, and the two animals had been at odds ever since. The cat kept stealing food from Lucy's bowl. Lucy hid the cat's toys. It was like having two children. But Jo liked having animals, and she had a feeling Sam did too.

Jo opened her laptop, her gaze sneaking to the icon for her personal files in the corner of the screen. Most of the information on her sister's case was on her other laptop at home, but this file had some general information on White Rock geography. She'd felt it was safe to keep it on her work laptop as there was really no indication it was part of her secret investigation. She opened the file, searching Google Images for the beech trees that she suspected marked the areas of shallow graves for victims similar to her sister. There were no beech trees on Frank Buckner's land.

Good. Wyatt was probably right. It was just a lost hiker. If Frank's dog had come home with the bone, it had likely been lying out in the woods, not buried in a shallow grave. She'd been in a panic for nothing. But now that those old feelings had surfaced, a new seed took root. Had she abandoned her sister's case prematurely?

CHAPTER FOUR

Lucy and Ranger hadn't gotten any friendlier since their standoff in Frank's backyard, but both must have sensed there was an important task at hand. They kept their distance from each other, trotting slightly ahead of everyone else into the woods.

Sam had notified the county sheriff, Bev Hatch, and she volunteered a few men for the search, but Sam had told her to give them a few hours. She wouldn't be able to mobilize that quickly anyway, and he held out hope that they would be able to find the bones easily. If it was a hiker who died of exposure, the rest of the bones should be close, unless animals had dragged some away. Sam hoped that wasn't the case. He wanted to save the county the trouble of a big search.

The mid-morning sun had warmed the air, and

even deep in the shadow of the woods it was hot and sticky. Sam lifted the rim of his baseball cap to brush the sweat from his forehead and then swatted a gnat with the cap before placing it back on his head.

Their presence had scared away most of the wildlife except for a few blue jays that watched them from the tops of tall pines and one brave squirrel that clung to the side of a tree about ten feet up, chattering at them noisily as they passed. Sam figured she was probably protecting a nest or a stash of acorns.

Beside Sam, Frank, who had his white socks pulled up over the cuffs of his pants to prevent ticks from climbing his legs, huffed and puffed to keep pace. He'd insisted on coming, pointing out that they needed Ranger to lead them to the area and he was the one who could best control the dog.

"Come on, boy, lead us to spot." Frank wheezed.

Sam and Wyatt exchanged a look. They'd been following the dog for ten minutes, and he seemed more interested in sniffing rocks and logs than leading them to where he'd found the bone. Truth be told, Ranger seemed kind of goofy, and Sam was questioning whether he had the wherewithal to find the spot again. Even Lucy seemed dubious, judging by the uncertain glances she kept casting back at Sam. But Lucy had sniffed the bone earlier in the car, and she was smart enough to know what they were looking for. She had a keen sense of smell. If more bones were around, she'd find them.

If animals had gotten to the bones, they could be spread about the forest, so Wyatt and Sam spaced themselves fifteen feet apart, each scanning the ground in front of them as they walked. A search would typically have more people spread out to cover a wider area, but at least this gave them a head start.

Up ahead, Lucy barked.

"They must have something," Frank surged forward with a burst of energy that belied his age.

They crested a small hill to find the two dogs on opposite sides of a tree. Lucy stood stock still, her ears straight, her tail hanging motionless, her gaze riveted on a patch of earth. Everything in her stance indicated that this was something important. Ranger wagged his tail, lunging back and forth. He ran to Frank, then back to the tree excitedly.

Sam stopped beside Lucy and gave her a pat on the head to let her know she'd done a good job. He scanned the area in front of them.

"I don't see any bones."

Lucy whined and pawed at the dirt. Maybe Lucy had just stumbled on a chipmunk's acorn stash or something else of canine interest. No, she wouldn't act so seriously if it was just that. But if she'd found the bones, where were they?

Sam didn't have a good feeling, and judging by the deep crease between Wyatt's brows, neither did he.

"Is this where you found that bone, boy?" Frank asked his dog. "Show us where the rest of them are."

Ranger barked and chased his tail in a circle. Lucy glanced over at him. Sam got the impression that if a dog could roll its eyes Lucy would've done so.

Sam studied the ground. If Ranger had found the femur here, other bones might be visible——unless he'd been finding the bones and dragging them off for a while. Maybe the femur was the last of them and the only one he decided to bring back home. Or maybe other animals had dragged off the rest of the bones. Still, the smaller bones from the hands and feet ... those should be here somewhere.

Sam kicked away a pile of wet leaves with his boot, disturbing a fire newt that wriggled off, seeking refuge under a rotted log. Instead of hard earth, the ground was soft. It had been disturbed, and claw marks ringed a shallow depression. Had Ranger dug the bone from here? It wasn't deep enough for the size of the bone, but something had clearly been digging. And Lucy stared at the hole.

Sam crouched down and gently brushed away more leaves. He didn't want to disturb the scene just in case. The moldy smell of wet leaves and the tang of damp earth wafted up as he worked, carefully brushing away clumps of earth as dark as coffee grounds and just as moist.

Ranger wasn't quite so gentle. He trotted to the other side of Sam and started clawing at the dirt.

"Whoa there boy, hold on!"

Lucy growled her disapproval of Ranger's actions, which only made him dig harder.

Rip!

Ranger jerked back his paw. A scrap of blue material was caught in his claw. Sam looked into the hole where he'd been digging. A tattered piece of shiny blue fabric reached up through the dirt. A tarp? His stomach plummeted.

Sam tugged on the scrap. It was stuck. Judging by the condition, it had been buried for quite some time. This corner must have worked its way up over time, but a larger section was buried deeper.

Ranger had worked the piece of tarp off his claw and resumed digging.

Sam shot his hand out to grab Ranger's collar.

"Hold up, boy." Sam glanced back at Frank. "Can you call him back?"

Frank craned his neck to look into the hole. "Sure. What do you think that is? Some kind of dump?"

Sam didn't think so, but he remained silent and focused on scooping out more dirt ever more carefully now so as not to disturb what they might find. Wyatt crouched down beside him to help. Lucy sat on the other side of the hole, her eyes flicking from the scrap of blue tarp to Sam and then to Wyatt.

About six inches down they hit a bigger section of tarp. Sam tugged on the edge. Even though it was full of small holes, it didn't budge. The material sure was strong. He cleared away enough to lift the corner. Underneath was a scrap of red plaid flannel and the unmistakable thin white shards of metatarsal bones. Human foot bones.

"Crap." Wyatt voiced what Sam was thinking and then took out his phone and started taking photos.

"Frank, you'd better take Ranger back to your house now." Sam glanced over his shoulder at the old man.

"What is it?" Frank strained to see what they'd uncovered. His eyes grew wide. "That ain't no old dinosaur, is it?"

"I'm afraid not." Sam stood and clapped Frank on the shoulder, studying him to make sure the realization of what they'd found wasn't too much for him. He saw steel in the old man's eyes. Frank was a tough old bird, like Sam's grandfather. He could handle it. "That bone you found wasn't a dinosaur bone, but it was something important. You need to let us take over now. Can you make it home okay by yourself?"

Frank tore his eyes from the shallow grave and looked at Sam. "Yeah. Sure, Sam." He turned reluctantly and started down the path, whistling for Ranger, who, fortunately, trotted obediently to his side. Even Lucy seemed relieved that the other dog was gone.

Sam turned back to the grave and studied what they'd uncovered, forming a plan of action in his mind. Wyatt was already taking photographs from all angles. That was good. Next they'd need to carefully uncover the rest.

He'd need crime scene markers and more evidence bags. He'd have to notify Bev Hatch right away and get John Dudley out here to look things over before they were disturbed. He had no idea how long this body had been buried or if any evidence had been preserved. But he knew one thing: Killers always leave clues. Sam's job was to find them.

Instead of uncovering the body of a missing hiker, now they were knee-deep in a crime scene. Sam wanted to make sure they processed it the right way. Someone was clearly inside that tarp, and finding out who, and what had happened to him or her, was even more important now.

"Guess this person just didn't wander off and get lost hiking," Wyatt said.

"Nope. Someone definitely put him or her in there, and we're gonna have to find out who."

CHAPTER FIVE

Jo tapped the eraser end of her pencil on her desk blotter and returned Major's glare as she waited for Kevin's brother. She couldn't wait to join Sam and Wyatt in the field to search for the bones of the lost hiker—and to clear her conscience by telling Sam about the private investigation she'd been conducting into her sister's disappearance.

Not telling him in the first place seemed so stupid now, but when she'd first arrived in town she had no intention of staying and no intention of opening up about her life. But she'd grown attached to the town. Attached to Sam. They'd formed a solid working relationship and friendship based on trust, and the more that trust grew, the more she felt like a traitor. It just became harder and harder to tell the truth, which was a shame because now that she knew Sam, she knew he'd be on board with doing everything he could to help her. He probably still would... once he forgave her.

"I'm here to see Detective Jody Harris," a male voice wafted from the reception area.

Kevin's brother. Right on time. Jo put the pencil down and stood as Reese led a tall, slightly nervous, dark-haired man around the post office boxes into the bullpen.

Reese gestured toward Jo. "Sgt. Jody Harris."

Jo stepped forward and held her hand out as Reese retreated back to the reception desk. The man switched a white plastic bag from his right hand to his left and clasped her hand. His handshake was warm and firm. His eyes held a hint of pain mixed with curiosity. "Brian Deckard. Kevin's brother."

"Thanks for coming. I'm sorry about your brother." Jo was sincere. She wondered if Kevin had been close with his brother. He'd never mentioned him, and Brian looked much older. She saw a slight family resemblance around the chin, but where Kevin was blond with light eyes, his brother was dark-haired with brown eyes. Half-brothers, maybe? Or maybe they didn't look much alike. Jo didn't look much like her sister, Bridget, but that was probably due to Bridget's haggard appearance from poor lifestyle choices. Still, she knew there were many siblings who bore no resemblance to one another.

Brian dropped her hand and glanced around the room. "Thanks. Me too."

"Have you been to the hospital? I visited him a couple days ago. I wasn't sure if there was an update." Jo hoped Brian would have optimistic news. The last time she'd visited Kevin the doctors had seen no change, but she was still hoping for him to pull through. Although they hadn't actually bonded from the start, Kevin had been a great officer. After all, he had taken a bullet for Lucy.

"Not really, but the doctor said there is some brain activity. I guess that's a good sign, but he also said it could be a long road." Brian scrubbed his hand through his cropped brown hair. "I think he was bracing me to not get my hopes up."

Jo scowled. "Don't think that way. Kevin is strong. He'll pull through."

"I hope so." They were silent for a few seconds as Brian's gaze flicked around the room. Then he held up a bag as if he just remembered he was holding it. "Oh, I brought these things. Some of his belongings that he had when he was admitted to the hospital. Seems like they should be at the police station. His badge. Computer stuff. Police T-shirt. It's all laundered."

Jo accepted the bag with a heavy heart. "Thanks. We'll keep these for when he comes back. And he will be back. Kevin's a hero in our eyes."

"So I heard. What exactly happened?"

Jo didn't see the harm in telling him what went down that night. The investigation was closed, the events a matter of public record. No sense in revealing the gory details, but she'd tell him enough to give him some closure on the events that put his brother in that hospital bed. "We were confronting a murderer, about to arrest him, when things went sideways. Our K-9 dog, Lucy, was in danger and Kevin jumped in front of her. He put himself in harm's way to save that dog."

"And the guy who shot Kevin is dead."

"Yep." Brian didn't look like the vigilante type, but maybe it was a good thing he didn't have someone to focus his anger on. Or maybe not. Would she feel better if she knew her sister's abductor was dead?

Brian gave a wan smile. "Kevin and I weren't that close. He didn't talk about his work much, but he did mention Lucy. He really liked her. I hope she wasn't harmed."

"She's fine. We love having her here at the station." A hissing came from the direction of the filing cabinets, and Jo glanced over. Major turned in a circle, fluffing his tail at her before curling in a ball. He tucked his face under his tail but left one watchful eye slit open, aimed in Jo's direction.

Brian didn't seem to notice. He was looking around the room again, his gaze stopping at each desk. Probably trying to picture his brother seated at one of them.

Jo pointed to Kevin's desk in the corner. "That one is your brother's."

Brian walked to Kevin's desk. Pens were scattered on the desktop. A keyboard sat in the middle, with a lined legal pad next to it. No one had the heart to remove anything from the desk, so the pad still had notes Kevin had taken to be typed into the system. Brian traced the writing with his forefinger then looked up at Jo.

"Was my brother working on any undercover investigations?"

Why would he ask that? A police force as small as White Rock's didn't conduct undercover operations. Those would be done by the county sheriff—unless it was personal, like Jo's investigation into her sister's disappearance. Or the off-record investigation she and Sam conducted into the death of their fellow officer, Tyler Richardson.

She was sure Kevin wasn't investigating anything. Not for the department, anyway. Sam would have told her. But there had been a time when she'd suspected Kevin was up to something. And just before the shooting, the killer had said something about Kevin working for the wrong side. But that had just been crazy talk by a cornered suspect, hadn't it? Of course it had. Kevin had jumped in the path of the bullet to save Lucy. And the last few months before that Kevin had proved himself more than trustworthy and loyal. "We don't really have much call for undercover work here. Why do you ask?"

Brian shrugged. "It's just that he seemed a little vague when I talked to him. Like he was working on something secret that he couldn't tell anyone about. It was probably nothing."

Yeah. Probably nothing. Because if Kevin *had* been working on some secret investigation, surely Sam would've told her, right? And besides what would he have been investigating? They didn't have much call for undercover work up here in northern New Hampshire. Kevin probably didn't want to spill any specifics to his brother, and he took that as being secretive.

"Well, I guess I should be going. Thanks for taking the time to talk with me." Brian shook her hand again and exited, leaving Jo clutching Kevin's bag.

She hurried to Sam's office to put the bag in Sam's closet so that it would be ready for Kevin's return.

She shoved the bag on the top shelf and grabbed a lime-green vest from the rack. With that task out of the way, her thoughts turned to assisting in the search and seeing with her own eyes that the bones were those of a lost hiker and had nothing to do with the monster who had taken her sister.

CHAPTER SIX

Jo coasted past the medical examiner's van and parked in front of the WRPD Tahoe on the dirt road near Frank Buckner's house. Sam had summoned John already? That meant they'd found the rest of the bones.

Sam had relayed the coordinates of the search site to Reese, and Jo had plugged them into a navigational app on her cell phone. The app was like a GPS that would direct her toward the coordinates. Now all she had to do was follow its directions through the woods.

The going wasn't easy. The site was on conservation land composed of acres of undeveloped forest that abutted Frank Buckner's property. She wasn't following a groomed trail, so she found herself navigating boulders, stumps and tree roots. At least the woods weren't dense, so she didn't have to battle too many low-hanging branches or bushes. It was only midmorning, but the nylon police vest didn't allow for circulation and sweat trickled down her back. The exertion from walking and the nerves that made her heart race didn't help. She probably shouldn't have had that third cup of coffee, either.

What would she find when she caught up with Sam? The remains of a hiker or something worse?

The humidity made her thick copper curls frizz. She got sick of pushing them out of her face, so she grabbed a band from her pocket and tamed them into a tight ponytail at the base of her neck.

As she came up a hill, she spotted Sam's tall frame first. He stood with his hands on his hips, looking down. Below him John crouched, working at something. Wyatt had his phone out, taking photos. This must be where they found the rest of the hiker's bones. But why did it look like John was a few inches below ground level? Had the hiker fallen into a ravine and been injured? Jo repressed a shudder at the thought of becoming injured during a hike and then slowly starving to death, delirious, in pain, and unable to fend off animals and bugs.

Sam glanced up at her approach. Her chest tightened at the grim look on his face. "How did things go with Kevin's brother?"

"Good..." Jo's voice trailed off as her eyes fell on what John was doing. It wasn't just a pile of bones lying on the forest floor. John was leaning into a six-inch-deep depression, meticulously scraping dirt like an archaeologist uncovering a rare find. Ivory-colored bones lay amidst scraps of red flannel. Only part of the skeleton was uncovered; the rest was still hidden under stringy remnants of bright blue tarp. This was no hiking accident. As Jo had feared, this was murder.

Jo stared at the bones. Though most of the skeleton was still covered by the tarp, she could clearly see the knee bone, femur and foot bones. She could also see that these were not the bones of a child. It wasn't her sister.

Relief washed over her, followed immediately by a wave of guilt. Even though it wasn't her sister, it was likely *someone's* sister. Some family had been missing this child for years. She knew how that hurt and how it could tear a family apart. Her heart ached for them.

"Kevin's brother?" Sam asked.

Jo tore her eyes from the bones to find Sam looking at her funny.

"Oh. Sorry. It went well. He just wanted to know what had happened and to drop off some clothes from the hospital and his badge." Jo's gaze flicked back down to the shallow grave. "So clearly this isn't a lost hiker."

"No. Didn't Reese tell you?" Sam brushed his hand through his short-cropped dark hair that had recently become peppered with gray. Jo had a few gray hairs creeping in herself, but where hers made her look old, Sam's made him look distinguished. "I guess maybe I didn't tell her. Been kinda busy here. Thanks for talking to Kevin's brother."

"No problem." Jo watched as John peeled back more of the tarp. "Any idea how old the victim was? Gender?"

"Hard to tell. I need to get the rest of the bones back to the lab to know for sure, but my guess is female, young adult." John gestured toward the top of the tarp. "You guys got enough photos of this? I want to push back more of the tarp."

"Yep," Wyatt said.

John slowly lifted another section of the tarp, careful not to dislodge what was beneath. It was important for them to see exactly how things were laid out.

"Where's Lucy?" Jo had thought something was missing. Now she realized it was the dog.

"She's off sniffing," Wyatt said as he crouched to take some close-ups.

"How long has she been here?" Jo gestured toward the grave. She used the pronoun "she," but John had said he didn't know for sure whether the skeleton was male or female. Something intuitively told her it was a female. Perhaps it was the delicate look of the bones or maybe the scraps of clothing or maybe just because she had thought of her sister.

"Hard to tell till I get things back to the lab, but I'm gonna guess maybe not less than three years, not more than ten. They weren't wrapped tight and the tarp didn't do much to preserve them. My guess is its main purpose was to move the body." John pointed to a clawed-up section of tarp. "See here? Looks like an animal dug here long ago and it got filled back in over time. Might not have the full remains underneath. The bugs have gotten in, and this earth is a little damp. As you know, the conditions of the ground have a lot to do with bone preservation. I'll take some soil samples back to the lab."

"Not much left for identification. Hopefully we'll be able to find out who it is from their dental records," Sam said.

"Hopefully."

Lucy barked from somewhere behind them, and they turned to see the wide brown brim of a Coos County sheriff's hat crest the hill. Bev Hatch was in her mid-fifties with shoulder-length salt and pepper hair and a don't-mess-with-me attitude. Her shrewd gray eyes took in the scene, sizing it up in seconds.

"So it's true. Not a hiker, a victim?" Bev glanced down at the grave and Jo knew she was cataloging it in her mind. Jo had worked with Bev before and liked the woman.

"Unfortunately, it is," John said.

John kept working the site, pulling the tarp away little by little, while Wyatt took photos.

Jo glanced across the grave, and her eyes met Sam's. His reflected empathy for the family and something else. Puzzlement? She guessed the puzzlement was for her. He was probably wondering why she looked so relieved. She never was good at masking her emotions. More guilt stabbed her. She needed to tell Sam about Tammy right away. But not here. She didn't want anyone but him to know about her sister. She'd tell him later back at the office when she could catch him alone.

"Huh, that's odd," John's voice jerked her attention back to the shallow grave. He'd peeled away most of the tarp and was looking down at the bones.

"What is?" Bev asked.

"I don't think this is the body you guys were looking for."

"How do you figure that?" Bev asked.

John gestured toward the tangle of bones near the feet.

"This one has both femurs. If I had to hazard a guess, this isn't the only shallow grave in the area."

WOOF!

Sam jerked his eyes away from the pair of femurs in the shallow grave to Lucy even as he was still trying to process John's revelation. More graves?

"So that's why she's been so busy sniffing." Wyatt was halfway toward Lucy. The dog stood stock still, her ears at attention, her tail motionless, eyes riveted on a patch of earth. "She must have smelled the other graves."

Lucy stood next to a fallen log. The log was rotted on the inside and mushrooms grew on the outside, but what was under it was of interest. Something had been digging, and Sam saw the unmistakable ivory-colored bumps of vertebrae.

"This must be where Ranger got the femur," Wyatt said. "Looks like it's all been dug up."

John pointed to the log. "This tree fell on top. It's a spruce, so it would decompose faster than most, but it's only partially rotted. I'd say that dates the graves to five years, give or take. 'Course the log could have rolled here." He squatted down and started brushing away dirt.

Wyatt started taking photos.

Bev squatted beside John.

Sam glanced around the woods. If there were two graves, could there be more? This *had* to be the grave with the missing femur, but still it didn't lessen the horror he felt. Some sicko had murdered people and buried them out here.

His gaze came to rest on Jo. She stood across from him, her eyes riveted on John's work. She was acting kind of odd. What was wrong with her? Had something happened with Kevin's brother that she didn't want to relate in front of everyone? Maybe he was just imagining it. He was a bit rattled after all. He hoped nothing else was going on. Two graves in one day was plenty.

"Looks like this might be another young female adult judging by the size of the pelvis. Possibly a teen." John gestured to a blank stretch of dirt between the thigh bone and the few small foot bones that were left. "Looks like someone grabbed the femur. This one is the body you were looking for."

"This grave is different," Bev said. "The bones are on top, not inside the tarp."

Sam squatted and brushed away some dirt to reveal the blue beneath. "But there is a tarp here. Maybe John was right about it being used to move the bodies and not so much to cover them. Either way, looks like we have our work cut out for us."

"We need to cordon off this area and search it thoroughly." Bev waved her left hand at the area between the two graves and pressed her phone to her ear with her right. "I'm calling Bill McGovern at the Staties. We need backup. I don't think we have enough people to processes this in a timely manner. We don't know how many graves are out here."

Sam nodded. He didn't relish the idea of a crowd with its hands in his investigation. More people meant more opportunities for screw-ups. But Bev was right. He, Jo, and Wyatt couldn't work this case on their own. It was too big. And it was too important to find out who these people were and notify their family members. And they'd need all the manpower they could muster to catch the killer.

His thoughts flitted briefly to his twin daughters. He couldn't imagine the anguish he'd feel if one of them disappeared. God forbid something like this happened to one of them. He wouldn't rest until he'd gotten justice. He was determined to do that for the family of the victims in these graves.

John had uncovered a skull. It lay apart from the rest of the bones. The earth dipped down into a depression, so it must have rolled away. It had come to rest in a pocket of reddish-brown clay-like dirt.

"Good. There's a jaw bone here." John bent further to inspect the bone, which was half buried in the clay. "No obvious dental work on this part." He brushed away more dirt to reveal the rest of the jaw. As Sam watched, a familiar pattern caught his eye.

"Hold on," Sam said.

John paused and glanced up at him. Sam leaned in. "That pattern of holes in the clay—it's the same pattern I noticed on the tarp in the other grave. Maybe it's preserved in the clay. I wonder if we can get this clump out in one piece. What do you think, Jo?"

Sam glanced up at his partner. Usually he and Jo operated on the same wavelength, but today she seemed distracted. She stared at the skull as if it would give her answers. "Jo?"

She jerked into motion. "Oh sure." Jo pulled latex gloves from her back pocket and got to work gently coaxing the lump of earth from the depression.

"That ties the two grave sites together," Bev had gone back to the first site to look at the holes. "If there was any doubt that two shallow graves in close proximity were tied together, the pattern of holes shows that the same person did this."

"What do you think it is?" Wyatt snapped a photo of the clay before Jo put it in a bag. "What made these holes?"

Sam shrugged. "I don't know. Some kind of aeration machine? You know, the kind that punches holes in lawns so the water can get deep into the roots."

"An aerator. But why would the killer use an aerator?" Jo glanced back at the bones. Had he been doing something creepy with the bodies?

"Maybe to irrigate the earth? To get it damper so the bodies would decompose faster," Wyatt suggested.

John glanced up at Bev. "Have the Staties bring some body bags. I'm going back to the first gravesite and finish that first. It's better preserved and we might have a better chance of finding evidence. This one's been ripped through by animals."

Sam followed John back to the first grave.

Wyatt joined them, zooming in on the pattern of holes that had been punctured through the blue tarp. "I didn't make anything of these at first, but you can see there's a pattern. Rows of holes and then there is a missing one every so often, as if the machine had something wrong with it."

"That's good. I guess that might be a way to identify it." Sam watched as John picked up little pieces of fabric and twigs with tweezers and deposited them in bags.

"We'll need more bags," John said.

"I'm on it." Bev still had her phone to her ear.

John tweezed a dried-out round leaf with serrated edges and held it up in the air. "That's odd."

"Is that a bog birch leaf?" Even in its desiccated state, Sam recognized the shape of the leaf. The rare shrub grew in only a few places in New Hampshire, and as far as he knew, this wasn't one of those places. The bog birch needed swampy ground to grow, and the forest they were in didn't fit the bill.

"I do believe it is." John glanced around. "I don't see any bog birches around here, though."

"Me either."

"What are you thinking?" Bev had come to stand at his elbow.

"The bodies were moved here." Sam said simply. "John was right. The tarps were used for dragging."

There was a commotion on the hill behind them, and Sam turned to see three green-uniformed state police officers cresting the hill along with someone he'd hoped he'd never see again: Holden Joyce from the FBI.

"Dammit." Bev muttered under her breath.

"My thoughts exactly," Sam said.

"What is *he* doing here?" Jo asked.

"Word must have gotten to them," Bev said. "More than one body. Shallow graves. That's serial killer territory. The FBI loves that shit."

The three of them stood and watched as Joyce approached. He was in his mid-fifties but tall and fit. He wore a tailored blue suit and a smirk on his face. They'd worked with Joyce before, and it had been less than pleasant. For some reason Holden Joyce had it out for Sam. He'd even accused him of being the killer in the last case he'd inserted himself into.

At least Holden couldn't accuse Sam this time. Unfortunately, Sam would have to play nice. He wouldn't do anything to impede the case, but he would do his damnedest to avoid any possibility of having to work directly with Holden.

He was thinking of an excuse to go back to the office early when his thoughts were interrupted by Lucy's sharp bark.

He pivoted to see her standing about fifty feet away. Her ears were straight up, her tail motionless. She peered at the ground with great intent, the same way she'd stood when she found the first two graves.

CHAPTER SEVEN

By the time they uncovered the third grave an hour later, the woods had become crowded with law enforcement. Deputies, state police, FBI. Jo counted twenty people combing the woods for more graves.

Jo searched with Lucy, helped John and the assistant medical examiners who had arrived on the scene with the remains in grave three, and avoided Holden Joyce.

She was dirty, hot, and slathered in noxious-smelling bug spray.

After they placed the final bone from grave three into the black plastic body bag, she stood and wiped her hands on her jeans. Scanning the area, she caught Holden Joyce staring at her.

The last case they'd worked had been a high-profile murder in which Holden Joyce had insinuated himself. She still wasn't exactly sure what the FBI interest in that case had been other than the fact that the victim had been a government official. Unlike Bev Hatch, Holden Joyce had been less than helpful. In fact, he tried to blame the murder on Sam. And he'd apparently had it out for Jo, as well. Joyce was not high on her list of allies even though he seemed to be processing this scene with care and compassion.

She'd caught Holden looking at her a few times during the morning, but instead of the accusatory glances he'd given her before these looks conveyed something different. Curiosity? Hope? It was almost as if he were sizing her up for some reason. Whatever it was, she could do without it.

Jo couldn't wait to get back to the station. She'd been relegated to the background now that the state police, sheriff's department, and FBI were here, and she was itching to do something productive. Even Lucy seemed bored. She'd stopped her meticulous sniffing half an hour ago and now just stood idly watching the team.

Jo made her way toward Sam, intending to ask if she could leave, but he spoke before she could reach him.

"It looks like the scene here is pretty much covered. I want to get back and start laying out some of this evidence and get going on a search for missing persons to see who these remains might belong to." Sam looked at her. "Will you stay until the search is completed?"

Damn! Sam had stolen her chance to escape. But her police training was such that she wouldn't argue or shirk her duties. Sam could count on her. So, she simply nodded and said, "Of course."

Sam rewarded her with one of his broad smiles. "Great. Thanks."

Holden glanced over from an area that he was searching with his team. "We can handle it, Mason. Bobby here is a trained K9 officer."

"I'm sure you can, but I'd like my sergeant to stay until we're done with the dog."

Holden shrugged and turned back to his search.

Bev had come to stand beside Jo, and they both watched Sam leave.

"How do you like that?" Bev asked, taking her Smokey Bear hat off and brushing the pollen off the brim. "Looks like Sam can't stand being around Holden Joyce either."

Jo crossed her arms over her chest. "Yeah, can't say I blame him."

"Me either," Bev turned to scowl in the direction of Holden. "I say this search is almost over anyway. Least I hope so. Hate to think of finding any more bodies."

"Me either." Jo turned to look at Lucy, who sat near the last grave. "I don't think we will. If there were more Lucy would still be sniffing."

"Yep. That's one smart canine. But of course Holden will want to see that for himself. He wouldn't want to admit that he's not as smart as a dog."

"What is that guy's deal, anyway?" Jo asked. Bev and Holden were around the same age, and she knew there had been bad blood between them before. She didn't want to pry, but any insight into Holden's odd behavior would be beneficial, especially if they had to work together on this case.

"He's got a hair up his ass," Bev said. "Case went bad on him early on and he's never gotten over it. It's a shame, too, because he'd actually be a good investigator if he didn't have such a chip on his shoulder. His ego won't let him get over that case."

"Too bad he keeps ending up on our cases."

"He likes these serial killer cases. I think it was this kind of case that broke him."

Jo remained silent. Something about the fact that Holden Joyce had messed up on a serial killer case pinged her radar. She stared at the large white FBI letters on the back of Holden's navy windbreaker.

Bev plopped her hat back on her head. "Well, better get to work. The sooner we finish combing the cordoned area, the better."

Jo wandered over to Lucy. She was certain there were no more graves. But she knew the rest of the team members would want to search to their own satisfaction. She snapped her fingers.

"Come on, girl. Let's get over to that last quadrant and see if we can dig anything up." They trotted behind the searchers who had spread out equidistantly in a line, their heads swiveling back and forth as their eyes combed the ground for signs of shallow graves.

Lucy stayed beside her, her head up in the air, sniffing the breeze and not at all concerned with the ground as she had been before the third grave was discovered. This behavior was further proof to Jo that there were no more graves to find.

Jo's mind wandered back to her sister Tammy. Had she been buried in a shallow grave like these? Her mind conjured images of tiny dirt-encrusted bones lying on a tattered blue tarp.

Thinking about Tammy spawned worries about her remaining sister, Bridget. Tammy's disappearance had ripped her family apart. Her mother had become consumed in grief, barely able to function. She died five years later. Her father had become a stranger. Jo hadn't seen him in a decade.

Bridget had only been twelve when it happened, but by the time she was sixteen she was experimenting with drugs. Now she was forty-two, and those years of drugs and living on the street had taken their toll. Jo had tried to help her get clean more times than she could count, but it never stuck. It was frustrating to keep trying, but she kept trying anyway.

She hadn't heard from Bridget in six months, which wasn't unusual. Bridget had no way to communicate other than the prepaid cell phones that Jo sent her, which were quickly "stolen" or "lost." But seeing these graves panicked Jo. If the victims were young as John had said, they wouldn't be her Tammy, but Bridget was just as vulnerable as these victims. She'd have to make a better attempt at contacting her.

Her mind back on the case, Jo thought about the photos she'd found inside the box that had belonged to fallen officer Tyler Richardson. Those photos had shown stripped beech tree branches. She'd once gotten a tip that the person who took her sister marked the graves by stripping the bark from the branches of the beech trees under which they were buried.

Those photos in Tyler's box had been taken here

in White Rock. But there were no beech trees in the area they were searching. And these graves were too new to belong to the same person who had taken Tammy. Or were they? Tammy had been taken thirty years ago, but Jo supposed her abductor could still be alive.

"Looks like you got yourself a pretty smart canine." Jo jumped at the voice. Holden Joyce had snuck up behind her while her thoughts had been on her sisters.

"We're lucky to have her." Jo wished Holden would go away, but he kept up with her.

"Serial killer cases can be nasty to work," he said.

"No doubt. Especially when it involves young women."

"Or children," Holden said softly.

Jo jerked her head to look at him. Something in his tone set her nerves on edge. "But these weren't children."

"No. Young adults. My guess is teen runaways. They're vulnerable and easy prey for sickos. There're no unsolved kidnappings reported in this area from the time that would coincide with these deaths." Again the tone, but Jo didn't look at him this time.

Jo shrugged. "Runaways or kidnap victims, either way the families will be devastated."

Holden was silent for a moment, then said in a low

voice almost as if to himself, "True. But don't you worry, we're gonna get the killer this time."

Holden's pace slowed, and he fell back a bit.

The tension in Jo's shoulders eased. There was an undertone to the conversation that she didn't understand. She wouldn't put it past Holden to have a hidden agenda, and she wanted no part of it.

"I think we're pretty much done with the search now. I don't think we'll find any graves further out from here. Lucy has good instincts. I'm calling it a day. You're free to go back to the station with her."

Jo snapped her fingers for Lucy and turned in the direction of the car, her eyes on Holden Joyce's retreating back. What was with all that serial killer talk? Was it just because of the current case, or did he know something?

Jo pulled out her cell phone and activated the GPS app to follow the trail back to where she'd parked. She needed to get back to the station and tell Sam everything about her sister's case as soon as possible.

CHAPTER EIGHT

Sam rummaged in the top filing cabinet drawer for push pins when he felt something staring at him. He looked up into a pair of golden eyes made even more brilliant by the jet black fur surrounding them. It was disturbing the way the cat stared at him, as if it knew something he didn't. It also disturbed him that the cat had crept closer to him while he'd been rummaging. He slowly extracted his hand with the box of pins and backed away.

"Don't worry, Major won't hurt you. He's just curious." Reese stood beside him, an array of papers clutched in her hand. "I've already done some research on missing persons over the last twenty years. John wasn't sure how long the bones had been there, so I figured I'd go wide. I've come up with a bunch of young adult females. Mostly runaways."

Sam took the papers and closed the filing cabinet gently. The cat still stared at him. It was unnerving. "I didn't realize the cat had a name."

Reese nodded. "We can't keep just calling him 'the cat,' so I figured I'd name him something police-like. Major Payne. It's a police rank and kind of fits his personality. He's had all his shots and everything. I mean, I assume we're keeping him, right?"

Sam glanced from her hopeful baby blues back to the cat. Major narrowed his eyes as if telling Sam they'd better keep him... or else.

"Yeah I guess we're keeping him." Sam knew the cat's previous owner was dead. He'd shot him. Sam felt responsible for the cat's homelessness, and he didn't have the heart to send him to the animal shelter.

Sam glanced down at the papers. So many runaways. They'd found three bodies, and he hadn't gotten a call about additional graves being discovered. Because of the way Lucy had acted he didn't think any more would be discovered. He wouldn't have left the scene if he did. He knew it would take the Staties and the FBI a while to figure that out on their own. Why subject himself to Holden Joyce's scrutiny any longer than he had to?

He felt bad about leaving Jo there, though. Jo had been acting a little off herself, and he'd wanted to swing by the Brewed Awakening drive-through to get her some jelly doughnuts. By the time he reached the store, they'd sold out of Jo's favorites.

Sam had bigger problems than jelly doughnuts and Holden Joyce. He had a killer on his hands. The fact that the graves were several years old didn't lessen the urgency for Sam. The killer might still be out there. He could've moved onto a different area, or he could be lying low until his next killing spree.

Sam had read that serial killers sometimes went dormant for years before starting up again. That wasn't going to happen on Sam's watch. He felt guilty enough that these crimes had likely happened during his tenure as chief. How had he not known that these brutal murders were taking place right under his watch? He owed it to the families and the victims to catch the killer.

This case took his mind off Lucas Thorne. The drug dealer who everyone accepted as a prominent real estate developer had been on Sam's radar for years. But Thorne was elusive, always getting someone else to do the dirty work, always a step ahead of the police. Sam had never been able to nail him for anything, and he'd tried hard.

Sam took the papers and push pins to the cork board on the back wall of the squad room. Reese, who had gone back to the lobby, appeared at his side, more papers in her hand. "Wyatt emailed these photos of the crime scene. I thought you might want them for the board, so I printed them."

"Thanks." Reese was turning out to be a great dispatcher and a big help around the station. She was still attending the police academy, so he couldn't make her an officer yet, but he hoped they would have an opening when she graduated. She'd already been vital in solving a few cases, and her contacts at the academy sure came in handy. Plus, she knew the routine. Like with the cork board. Maybe some would think it old fashioned, but Reese knew it was part of Sam's process and respected that.

Reese went back to the front desk, and Sam got to work laying the photos out in an order that made sense to him. When he was done, he stood back so he could take them all in at once.

Dirt-smudged bones, snatches of bright blue tarp, the weird pattern of holes, the bog birch leaf. The leaf was the big lead as far as he was concerned. These girls had been killed at a different location, and Sam needed to figure out exactly where that location was.

"The search is breaking up." Wyatt had come in and was now standing beside him studying the photos. "No other graves found."

"Well that's a relief. Kind of figured when Lucy stopped sniffing."

"Me too."

Sam turned around and frowned. "Where are Jo and Lucy?"

"She was talking to Holden Joyce when I left. Bill McGovern gave me a ride back."

Sam turned back to the photos. He tapped the one of the leaf and scrolled to the information page on his cell phone where he'd looked up the bog birch earlier just to be sure. He held the phone up to the photo. "I think this is a big clue. The bog birch is incredibly rare in New Hampshire. We need to figure out if it grows anywhere near here."

"I'm on it." Wyatt quickly headed to his desk.

Wyatt was eager to help. Sam couldn't blame him. He was new in the department, and they hadn't exactly included him in the last takedown mostly because they hadn't worked with him much and Sam wanted him to have more experience before they had to rely on each other in a dangerous situation. But Wyatt was turning out to be a smart cop. Sam was confident that he would be a valuable addition to the team.

The lobby door opened, and Lucy bounded into the squad room. She stopped beside Sam, who bent to pet her. Atop the filing cabinet, Major hissed, and Lucy side-stepped to the other side of Sam. Jo followed closely behind. Dirt smudged her nose, and a strand of her coppery hair had escaped the confines of her pony-tail to coil around her face.

"They're done. Only three graves. Lucy did a great job." She went over to her desk and reached into the drawer, pulling out a treat that she tossed in the air. Lucy jumped up and caught it in her mouth. Major did more hissing.

Jo turned to him. "You haven't done anything, so I'm not giving you a treat."

"Don't be mean to him, he's very sensitive," Reese yelled from the lobby.

Jo turned to Sam, her hands on her hips. "Thanks for leaving me stuck with Holden Joyce."

Sam cringed. A jelly doughnut peace offering would really come in handy right now. "Hey, that's a benefit to being the boss."

Jo rolled her eyes, but she was smiling. Sam felt relieved. Jo was just teasing. And now she didn't seem as distracted as she had when they were out in the woods, but her eyes kept darting toward his office.

Maybe something had happened out there that she wanted to tell him about privately. Did it have to do with her meeting with Kevin's brother? That would explain her odd behavior at the crime scene. Or maybe something had happened with Holden Joyce. He wouldn't be surprised if the guy had somehow concocted some twisted reasoning that made Sam the perpetrator in these killings. He should probably make up an excuse to get in the office and hear her out, but he didn't want Wyatt to think something weird was going on between them. Maybe he could think up a—

"Hey, Sam, you ready for a lunch date?"

Lunch date? Crap. Sam had forgotten all about that.

Marnie Wilson came around the post office boxes, Reese following behind her with a sour look on her face. Marnie had probably breezed right past the dispatcher, who liked to protect them from unannounced visitors.

Sam glanced back at the cork board. He didn't have time for lunch. He was in the middle of an important investigation.

"Sorry, Marnie, I forgot all about it. I don't think I have time. We just discovered..." He didn't really want to tell Marnie Wilson the details. They would be all over the news shortly, but he didn't think it was a good idea to be telling the general public about the case. Even though Marnie was running for mayor, she was still just a civilian.

"Oh," Marnie's face fell, her eyes drifting to the cork board. "I'm sorry. Harry said that I should come by and I just..."

Darn it. Harry had said this would be a personal favor to him. Guilt crushed Sam's resolve. He'd given Harry his word, and Marnie had made a special stop.

He supposed it was his duty as chief of police to find out what Marnie was about. With the former mayor dead and the acting mayor someone Sam definitely did not want in office, he needed to figure out who he should put his vote behind.

He didn't know much about Marnie. What were her causes? Would she give the police department the necessary funding? Harry liked her because she was for senior citizens' programs. But what else was she for? Or against, for that matter?

This investigation could go on for a long time. If ever there was a time to take a break, it was now because they only had one lead and Wyatt was working on it. Until he discovered where the bog birch shrub grew, Sam didn't have much to do but think.

And he could think over lunch as well as anywhere else.

"Why not go, Sam?" Wyatt asked. "We still need more information from John, and I'm following up that lead. I think we've got it covered, right, Jo?"

Jo, now seated at her desk, the eraser end of her pencil tap-tap-tapping on the wooden surface, her face expressionless, muttered, "Yeah, of course we've got it covered. Go ahead." Did he detect a hint of annoyance?

Sam glanced back at the cork board, then at scowling Reese. He had the distinct impression that Reese did not like Marnie Wilson, but he had no idea why.

He could never figure women out. Was it jealousy? Marnie was a handsome woman in a no-nonsense kind of way. She was about the same age as Sam, maybe a little older, but well preserved. Attractive. Not that Sam was looking. After two failed marriages he didn't want to go down that road again, especially not with someone running for mayor. But he was getting hungry, and he supposed he should hear her out. And it would appease Harry.

"Okay. But I can't take a long time. You know, public servant and all."

"Of course not. I totally understand," Marnie

hooked her arm through his. "I already have a reservation at Silo's."

Sam looked back over his shoulder as Marnie propelled him toward the lobby. "Wyatt, text me the minute you find anything."

CHAPTER NINE

Jo's gaze drifted to Reese as Sam and Marnie disappeared around the bank of brass post office boxes. Judging by the look on the dispatcher's face, she didn't like Marnie Wilson any more than Jo did.

Jo wasn't even sure what she didn't like about the woman. It was just a gut feeling. She hadn't talked to her much, but Jo felt as though Marnie was one of those who told you what you wanted to hear. She was a politician, after all, and wasn't that the way with all politicians?

Maybe it was just Jo's aversion to politics that made her feel Marnie couldn't be trusted. It certainly didn't have anything to do with the way she was obviously flirting with Sam. Sam and Jo were friends, nothing more, though she didn't want to see her *friend* get caught up with someone untrustworthy. She thought Sam had better instincts.

What was this business about a date, anyway? In the middle of the day? In the middle of a case? Sam had looked surprised when Marnie came waltzing in. More than likely it wasn't a date but something arranged by Harry Woolston. Harry had been trying to get Sam to talk to Marnie for months now. This was pretty bad timing, but better now before they got involved in chasing down leads.

Jo pushed away her disappointment. She'd wanted to tell Sam about her sister before things really started to heat up. She'd have to wait for another opportunity. Maybe Sam wouldn't even want to be bothered about her old case with this mess on his hands. Still, she should tell him. Even though it had nothing to do with the current case, it was the right thing to do, if only to stop the guilt of not being totally straight with Sam.

As if sensing Jo's conflicting thoughts, Lucy came over and put her head in Jo's lap, looking up at her with warm brown eyes. The dog had an uncanny knack of knowing when someone needed a little comfort.

"You did a good job today." Jo stroked the soft fur on Lucy's forehead.

"It's a lot of work running around in the woods. She's probably hungry." Reese reached into the cabinet above the coffeemaker for Lucy's bowl and food. The sound of kibble clanking on stainless steel caught Lucy's attention. And Major's, too, judging by the way he stood and stretched his long legs in front of him, his eyes glued to the bowl.

Reese placed the bowl in the corner where they usually fed Lucy.

Meow!

Major leapt from the filing cabinet, raced to the bowl and immediately started chowing down.

"Hey, that's Lucy's food! You have your own." Reese pulled a smaller bowl out of the cabinet along with a can of cat food. The metallic sound of the pop tab top caught the attention of Lucy, who had been standing a few feet away from Major as if afraid to approach him. Lucy had already suffered a bloodied nose from Major's razor-sharp claws, and apparently even defending her dinner wasn't enough to make her want to repeat the experience. Major kept eating, unfazed by the opening of the can. Apparently he preferred dog food.

Lucy flicked pleading eyes at them.

"I'll distract him for you, Lucy." Wyatt opened his drawer and took out a mouse-shaped toy. He approached Major cautiously, dangling the toy by its tail in front of him. At the sight of the mouse, Major lifted his head, and his tail swished back and forth. Suddenly his paw shot out. He skewered the mouse, knocking it out of Wyatt's hand. The mouse flew through the air. Major scampered after it, catching it and rolling to the ground.

Lucy approached her bowl with one eye on Major.

Reese added some more food to make up for what the cat had stolen.

"Looks like you have Major's number," Jo said.

Wyatt shrugged. "I think he likes me. Maybe because I wasn't there when everything went down with his owner. You gotta feel sorry for him. Everything he knew has been uprooted and he's in unfamiliar territory. He's probably just trying to figure out how he fits in."

Jo's estimation of Wyatt ticked up a notch. Anyone who was an animal lover couldn't be half bad.

Wyatt was right about the cat. The poor thing was in unfamiliar territory, probably uncertain of its fate. She felt sorry for Major and vowed to be kinder toward him, to let him know he was among friends. Her thoughts drifted to the cat that had been appearing on the porch of her small cottage. That cat wasn't overly friendly either. She'd been trying to earn its trust by putting out treats and not trying to pressure it too much. Maybe the same tactics would work with Major.

"Well, you sure know how to distract him." Reese pointed toward the cat, now flopped in the corner and rolling around with the mouse, ignoring Lucy's food.

"It could be the catnip I put inside the toy." Wyatt smiled and waggled his brows. It was the first time she'd seen him joke, and Jo noticed that he was really kind of cute when he smiled. He was too young for her by about ten years, but it was nice to know he had a sense of humor and was starting to feel comfortable enough around them to show it.

"Hey, whatever works." Jo watched the cat as he padded to the plush cat bed in the corner with the toy in his mouth. He circled the inside of the bed, then plopped down. He looked comfortable. "Maybe we should get catnip toys for all of us. They seem to have a calming effect and this case is going to be a doozy."

Wyatt's gaze drifted from the cat to Jo. She saw a determined, steely look in his green eyes. Was he studying her a little too closely? No. She was getting paranoid after all the questions Holden Joyce had asked.

"You can say that again. Don't worry, though, we'll find out who did this. We have to."

WYATT COULD TELL he was earning points with his colleagues by the way he'd handled Major. The cat hadn't exactly been the friendliest creature he'd ever seen, but he figured it was with good reason. He was adjusting, just as Wyatt was.

Wyatt was starting to feel more comfortable in White Rock. He could tell that Sam and Jo were starting to trust him. But he also sensed a weird undercurrent between them. Mostly with Jo. She'd acted off at the search site this morning, and then when she'd returned to the station he got the distinct impression that she was jittery about something. Maybe she had a secret too.

But even if she did have a secret, he felt confident that she and Sam really cared about this case. They were good cops. Cops with compassion. Cops who cared about justice. Not all cops felt that way, as Wyatt had discovered early in his career.

A surge of pride bubbled up inside him. Looking into where the bog birch shrubs grew was the first important task Sam had entrusted to him. That was a sign that Sam saw him as an important part of the team.

As disturbing as this case was, he wanted to be a big part of investigating it. That might help him atone for things and prove that he wasn't a product of his lineage.

That atonement was important to him because when it came right down to it, that was why he'd come to the small northern New Hampshire town—to right wrongs. In a small-town department he'd get a chance to do real investigative work. Not be relegated to traffic duty as he had been in the city.

Plus, the pace and laid-back lifestyle in White Rock suited him. The people were nice. Friendlier than in the city, for sure. The rolling mountains, lush valleys, and sparkling lakes and streams were a welcome break from expressways and skyscrapers.

And working with Lucy was an added perk. He'd become quite attached to the dog in the short time he'd been here. He even liked having Major at the station, even though the cat was less than companionable. You'd never see a cat in a big city police force, but everyone knew animals helped with stress. Right now the tension between Lucy and Major was *causing* a little stress. Wyatt was sure it would all smooth over eventually.

Wyatt had been disappointed not to be included when they tracked down the mayor's killer. If Sam had included him, things might've gone differently. Maybe Kevin Deckard would be sitting at his desk right now instead of lying in a hospital bed.

But he understood why Sam hadn't included him. He was new, and Sam was still feeling him out. In intense situations like that, it worked best to have fellow officers whose actions and motivations you were familiar with because often one had to react on instinct and had to be able to anticipate the other officers' reactions.

He'd gained some level of acceptance now, which was good. He wasn't going to sit back and relax, though. He had to do good work and to earn his keep, as his mother had always told him.

Lucy finished her meal without incident. Major was zonked out in his bed, the catnip mouse between his paws. Lucy cast him a weary glance before trotting into Sam's office, no doubt to seek out the patch of afternoon sun that slanted through the large windows.

Major let out a snore. It looked like the cat was feeling more at home, just as Wyatt was. The two of them were on the same track.

Wyatt turned back to his computer. He didn't want to waste any time. Finding the location of the bog birch might reveal where the victims were killed. And if they could discover where the victims had been killed, they might find clues that would lead them to the killer. This might be the most important task of the case and perhaps the most important of his entire career thus far.

CHAPTER TEN

S am fiddled with his fork and silently cursed Harry. He'd rather be back at the station or out fishing or just about anywhere but sitting with Marnie Wilson in a fancy restaurant. Never mind that he had an important case; he wasn't exactly the fancy restaurant type. Give him a burger and a beer at the local watering hole and he was happy. But he'd promised Harry, and Sam kept his promises. At least he was getting this over with.

Marnie paused from her monologue on how she'd come to settle in White Rock as the waitress deposited a basket of bread on the table and refilled their tall thin tumblers with water.

"So what about you? How did you end up here?" Marnie asked after the waitress departed.

"Born here." Sam sipped his water and scanned the restaurant with a cop's eye, looking for potential trouble. Not that he expected any, it was just habit. Years of training had wired him to always be vigilant.

The restaurant was one of those upscale rustic places. It was in an old mill, some walls with original brick, the others covered in old barn board right up to the twenty-foot-high ceilings, which had exposed duct-work and plumbing painted black so it all blended.

The booths were large and comfortable, faux leather and blue, green and brown patterned fabric. Sam supposed the fabric was trendy, but to him the colors didn't match. His tastes ran more to plain brown and green. The tables were all draped in white linen, silverware gleamed, and crystal wine glasses sparkled.

It was mid-afternoon, so the restaurant was nearly empty. One couple sat a few tables away, speaking in hushed tones. Five men were seated at a round table in the corner, several drinks in front of them. The conversation was boisterous. Sam figured them for salesmen having a long lunch, possibly celebrating a big sale.

"That's nice. I imagine being a local is a big advantage for the chief of police," Marnie said.

Sam's gaze drifted back to Marnie. He supposed she was pretty, but not in an obvious way. Her nose was a little too big, her face a little too round, and her eyes a little too green. She had her shoulder-length honey-blond hair pulled back in a ponytail that was a little too casual.

He liked that she dressed in jeans and T-shirts. It made her seem less stuffy. Then again, she was running for mayor. The casual hair and outfits might be strategic to appeal to the common man. She seemed nice enough, though, and Sam might have fostered the dull spark he felt in her presence if she'd been anyone else but a candidate for mayor.

"I suppose it is an advantage. I do know a lot of folks." Sam had never thought about it as an advantage. He loved White Rock and had always wanted to be chief so he could help the town.

Knowing a large percentage of the population meant he could give them personal attention. They were nice folks. Except for the person who had put those girls in the graves. Was that person still in town? It didn't matter. Sam would find him no matter where he was and bring him in.

In fact, he should be back at the station right now figuring out just how to do that. He glanced down at the phone he'd put on the seat of the booth beside him. No text from Wyatt yet. He supposed he could suffer here a few more minutes, at least until he finished his lunch.

The waitress came and slid their meals onto the table. A burger for him; some salad concoction for Marnie. Rabbit food. Sam lifted the top of the brioche bun and cut into the burger. Medium rare, just the way he liked it. The smell of charred beef wafted up and his stomach grumbled. He had to admit, the over-priced burger did smell good.

"This looks delicious." Marnie picked through her salad with a fork like an old lady picking through a box of chocolates for her favorites.

"Sure does." Well, at least the burger did. Sam frowned at the side of coleslaw he'd ordered because the restaurant didn't serve french fries.

Marnie nibbled a piece of lettuce. "I'm sure Harry told you that even though I'm not originally from town I *am* dedicated to helping White Rock and its people. Especially the seniors."

"Yeah, Harry is excited about the senior citizen programs that you support." Sam took a bite of the burger. It was juicy, and the horseradish sauce provided a perfect tangy complement to the cheese. Maybe this place wasn't so bad after all.

"Not just seniors. I want to help everyone in town." Marnie speared a grape tomato and popped it in her mouth.

Sam cut to the chase. There were only a few things

he was interested in when it came to the town, and she might as well know what they were right away. "What about the construction that's going on in town? Do you plan to do anything about that?"

"You mean Thorne Enterprises and Mervale?" Marnie asked.

"You must have seen new hotels and strip malls sprouting up. This is a small town. It should retain the small-town charm."

"I agree." She focused on her salad. Afraid to look him in the eye or just picking out the good stuff?

"So, if you were mayor you'd make sure that permits for new construction were issued with more restraint?"

"Well, *some* new construction is good for the town. It provides jobs. And hotels will bring in more tourists, and that helps local business."

"It's becoming overdeveloped. Not only that, but their tactics are underhanded. They wait for the old folks who owned the farms to die off and then try to steal the land right out from under their heirs, often offering way below market price."

Marnie frowned. "I don't condone underhanded tactics. I'm sure Beryl would not approve of that. Are you sure that's what Thorne is doing?"

"Beryl? Oh, you mean Thorne's wife?"

Marnie nodded. "She's a lovely woman."

Sam doubted anyone married to Thorne would be lovely. Hadn't Harry said that Thorne's wife wore the pants in the family? Now that he recalled, it was the wife who had all the money. Her family wealth had funded Thorne's construction business. "Surely his wife must know about his nasty tactics. I heard his business is funded by her family money. She must know what's going on."

"Not necessarily. It's true Beryl's family is loaded with old money. They were real estate developers for generations. When she met Lucas, they brought him into the business, and when they married they helped him go out on his own. But that doesn't mean she knows everything that's going on. She actually works for her family business still, not with her husband." Marnie chuckled. "You know how it is; sometimes working together and being married just doesn't work out. Anyway, she's much too interested in her environmental causes to keep such a close eye on her husband."

"Environmental causes?"

"Yes. She's taken quite an interest in those Great Bearded Owls."

"No kidding." Earlier that summer, a species of owls previously believed to be extinct had been discovered in White Rock. Their nesting place was adjacent to a new hotel that Thorne was building.

Experts had worried that the construction would disturb the owls. They'd tried to get the project shut down, but somehow Thorne had finagled things to continue.

Marnie nibbled more lettuce. "While I do approve of some new construction in the name of progress, I am dedicated to keeping the town as pristine as possible."

Sam's eyes narrowed. Political doublespeak. Marnie was only telling him what he wanted to hear. "That's not the only problem the town has with Thorne. I'm sure you are aware of the drug problem."

Something flickered in her eyes. She knew. Anyone running for mayor would be up on that.

Sam continued, "It's a big concern of mine. And I'd be likely to throw my support behind the candidate who was going to help put the leader of the drug ring away and not hinder our investigations by blocking search warrants."

"Of course I wouldn't hinder that. What mayor would?"

Sam snorted. "You'd be surprised."

Marnie looked at him curiously, then leaned across the table. Sam got a whiff of flowery perfume. His nose twitched, and he suppressed a sneeze. "I'm sure you've heard of the Convale project."

Was she changing the subject? Of course he'd heard of it. Convale was a big power company out of Canada trying to make inroads to supply power to the upper states. The only problem with that was they had to go through New Hampshire with their gigantic unsightly power lines to get there. Sam had heard that White Rock was in the proposed path. That wasn't something Sam would ever get on board with, but the project was still in its infancy. Everything was hush-hush, with very little information available.

"I have. They want to litter the White Rock scenery with power lines." Sam took another bite of burger. He glanced down at his phone again. No text. He would have to make an excuse to leave. The investigation was much more important than listening to Marnie Wilson's rhetoric. And if she was trying to persuade him to get on board with the Convale project, their friendship was about to come to an abrupt end.

"No, it's not like that. It would only be in remote sections that no one could even see, deep in the forest. It would bring a lot of money to the town. And there may be other ways than having tall towers."

"So you're not opposed to it?" She wouldn't get his

support, then. But who did that leave? Jamison, the acting mayor? Henley Jamison probably wasn't opposed to it either.

Marnie sat back in her seat. "Well, I *am* opposed to ruining the pristine landscape."

"That we can agree on." Sam took the last of his burger. There was something to be said for fancy beef. It was probably the best burger he'd ever had.

As he chewed, Marnie picked at her salad and babbled about how she had formed this committee and that committee in her efforts to preserve wildlife and land.

Sam's thoughts drifted back to the case. He didn't really care what Marnie had done. He was more interested in what she was *going* to do and what she stood for. Judging by this conversation, he was doubtful as to whether they aligned with the things he stood for.

"... I couldn't help but notice the photos in the police station. And Frank Buckner was downtown talking about some bone his dog found. I saw the state police and county sheriff driving out toward his place. I assume a big case is in the works."

When had the conversation turned to that? Sam wanted to contain the details of the case as long as possible, but in a small town like White Rock word got around fast. "Sadly, some remains were found in the woods."

"Some?"

Sam nodded grimly. She'd already seen the photos, and he was sure word was out about more than one grave, especially with the amount of manpower they'd had out searching. "Unfortunately, more than one. It looks like I'm going to have my work cut out for me, which is why—"

Ding!

Sam's eyes jerked to his phone. Wyatt had located the bog area in a small town an hour away.

He pushed up from the table, pulled out his wallet, and threw some cash down. "Sorry. I hate to cut things short, but we have a break in the case and I need to get back to the station."

CHAPTER ELEVEN

"I see the Tahoe parked up ahead."

Sam lurched sideways as Bev hit another pothole on the barely navigable path that passed for a dirt road. He was starting to regret agreeing to let her pick him up so Wyatt and Jo could head out ahead in the Tahoe. Bev was about the worst driver he'd ever ridden with.

He peered through the bug splatter on the windshield, barely making out the back end of the Tahoe through the thick foliage ahead.

The Tahoe was pulled to the side as much as possible. To the east was a swampy area. Lucy, Wyatt, and Jo were outside, inspecting the vegetation. Sam recognized several swamp-loving plant varieties, including the bog birch.

This had to be where the killer had claimed his victims.

Lucy trotted over as Sam got out of the SUV. Somewhere a frog croaked, providing the perfect accompaniment to the rank smell of the swamp and the staccato buzz of the insects. Out here, the foliage was dense, and the woods had a yellowish-green cast as the afternoon sun struggled to filter through a dense canopy.

"You think this is the place?" Bev asked.

"This is the only known area with this species of bog birch within driving distance of where we found the bodies," Wyatt said.

"Has to be it." Sam said. "The kill site would have to be within driving distance of White Rock. The killer would want to be able to transport the bodies easily and quickly."

"Why even bother? This place is remote enough. He could just bury them here." Bev gestured toward the wetlands a few feet beyond the parked Tahoe. "Or throw them in the swamp. No one would come digging around here."

"But why here? I mean it is remote, but is there some special association for the killer? We need to figure out who owns this." Sam pulled his phone out and zipped off a text instructing Reese to look up the property records.

"I think I might know why." Jo pointed to a break in the tall grasses that surrounded them. A trail? It was so narrow it could have been a deer trail, or maybe it had once been wider and had grown in because it hadn't been used in a long time. Lucy started up the trail, and the rest of them followed. As they got further into the woods the trail widened. Definitely bigger than a deer trail.

They walked silently, accompanied by the sucking sounds of the mud trying to pull off their boots and the incessant buzzing of insects. Lucy trotted ahead, leaving paw prints in the thick mud.

After about five minutes, Bev slowed, her gray eyes zeroing in on something. "Hold up." She squinted ahead. "What's that through the trees?"

The woods were dense, but Sam made out a square shape through the trunks and leaves. A small cabin. Sam's heartbeat kicked up a notch, and he pulled out his gun.

"We need to approach cautiously."

They walked slowly, careful not to step on any twigs, their guns out and ready. As they got closer, Sam noted the dilapidated cabin sat on top of a small knoll about twenty feet from a marsh. The brown siding was falling off near the back. A mattress and other debris littered the outside near a rusty propane cylinder. The yard was overgrown with grass and shrubs. A trumpet vine wound its way around the chimney, thick with green leaves and orange flowers. The screens on the porch were all ripped. If anyone was living in there, they sure weren't living the high life.

"You think anyone's in there?" Bev asked.

"I hope not." Wyatt eyed the cabin cautiously.

As they approached, Sam tensed, ready to spring should anyone rush out at them.

Lucy kept her distance. Did she sense someone inside? Sam's eyes darted from one window to the other, looking for any movement that would indicate someone was inside.

The screen door hung open, half off one hinge. It squeaked eerily as a slight breeze moved it, but that was the only movement or sound that came from the cabin.

Wyatt was the first to reach the porch steps. He looked at them over his shoulder as he raised his gun straight in front of him. "Cover me."

The first step squeaked, and everyone tensed, but no one came rushing out. Wyatt made it up onto the porch without incident, and they all relaxed.

"You guys gotta see this." Wyatt was on the porch

looking in through one of the windows. Sam stepped up beside him, peering through a layer of dirt.

The interior of the cabin was a wreck. Stained mattresses littered the floor. Junk food wrappers battled dirty pieces of clothing for floor space. Wallpaper hung from water-stained walls. In one room—the living room, Sam guessed—the ceiling had collapsed into the room. In the corner a vine grew down into the room. Thick dust covered every surface.

Sam relaxed. It was obvious that no one was inside.

Jo's hand was on the door knob. "It's open."

"Let's go in." Sam holstered his gun and pulled out some latex gloves. "But be careful about touching or moving anything. If this cabin belonged to the killer, this could be a crime scene."

The cabin smelled musty, and there was a sour ammonia-like tang in the air. Urine? Sam glanced over his shoulder. Lucy stood in the doorway, her nose twitching.

"You stay out there, Lucy." She backed up and sat, her head swiveling between the yard and them.

Wyatt started taking photos. Sam scanned the mess for evidence that the killings had taken place there. Hard to tell with all the debris.

"I don't see any blood or obvious signs of murder, but we don't know how the victims died. He could have strangled them. Or killed them outside. Or maybe this isn't even where they were killed," Bev said.

"This clothing, maybe some of it belonged to them. There wasn't much in those graves," Sam said. "Let's make sure we get photos that family members might be able to identify."

"I don't see any signs of this place being recently inhabited," Wyatt said.

"Who could live like this?" Jo asked as she made her way into the hallway.

"A serial killer?" Bev suggested.

"If he was here, he's long gone." Wyatt said.

"Maybe not *just* a serial killer..." Jo stood just down the hallway, in the doorway to another room, her back to them as she spoke.

Sam walked over and looked into the room over her shoulder. The kitchen hadn't been used much for cooking... at least not for cooking food.

The counters were strewn with rubber hosing. Empty rolls of duct tape lay on the floor. Glass containers sat on the rusted-out stove. Dozens of empty foil pill packets were piled in the corner.

Sam's gaze met Jo's. "An abandoned meth lab?"

JO EYED the debris in the kitchen. It clearly hadn't been used in years but had all the markings of the remains of a meth lab. The beakers, chemicals and funnels were gone, but what had been left behind were the scraps of what one would find. The old Sudafed containers in the corner were a dead giveaway. And that explained the slight smell of ammonia she'd noticed when they'd entered.

She looked at Sam. "Why do you think it was abandoned?"

"Hard telling. They didn't get busted, that's for sure. Everything would have been taken for evidence. Maybe they went out of business or just picked up stakes and moved on."

"You think it's Thorne?"

"Could be. It's pretty far from his territory, but I guess it makes sense not to have something like this in his own backyard," Sam said.

"He might've ceased operation when things heated up with the Dupont investigation." Bev had come to stand between them and was eyeing the debris in the kitchen.

Jo squinted at the thick layer of dust on the scarred counters and the cobwebs that hung in every corner. "I don't know. That was just a few months ago. This place looks like it hasn't been touched in years."

"You think it has something to do with the bodies?" Bev asked.

Sam ventured into the kitchen and started opening the cabinets. "Could be. The timeline could be right. But a serial killer who cooks meth?"

Wyatt had come to stand behind Bev. He let out a low whistle. "Is this what I think it is?"

"Yep. Better get some photos before the feds come in and mess everything up. There could be something here that links to Thorne or to those bodies." Sam turned around and looked at the room. "We need to do this by the book. There will be all kinds of police units with their fingers in this pie. This will be a high-profile case, but it could finally be our chance to get Thorne, and we don't want him to get off on a technicality because some evidence wasn't handled properly."

Wyatt stepped into the room, squatting to get close-ups of the debris on the floor.

"Be careful, though," Bev cautioned. "We don't know what kind of chemical substances are lingering in here."

Sam glanced at the door. "Good point. Where's Lucy?"

"She's outside guarding the front steps," Wyatt said.

"Good. Let's make sure she doesn't come in."

Jo followed Sam and Bev back to the living room, her eyes scanning the debris.

"The only missing persons we have are runaways. I assume that's who were in those graves. Runaways often fall victim to drugs and prostitution." Bev's gray eyes flashed with anger. "Some sick predator could've taken advantage of that."

"You think we might find some clothing from the victims here?" Jo asked.

"It's a long shot, but we don't want to overlook anything that can tie those bodies to the meth lab."

Jo's heart squeezed. Thorne *had* to be behind this. But was he a drug dealer *and* a serial killer? Somehow it didn't make sense. Because of the investigation she'd been conducting into her sister's disappearance, she'd been tuned into serial killer activity for years. Never once had Thorne pinged on her radar. She'd not seen any evidence of it in anything he'd done the five years she'd worked here. Then again, her investigation had brought her to White Rock while following leads the police didn't deem important enough to follow. Was it possible there was a connection to Thorne?

"We'd better clear out." Bev took out her phone. "I'm going to notify the state police and get their hazmat unit up here."

"Wait until Holden Joyce hears about this one."

Sam came in from the kitchen and stripped off his gloves. "We'll never get rid of him now."

Bev rolled her eyes and scrolled through her contacts. "This certainly is a unique case. I'm sure the FBI will be interested."

"Yeah, maybe we can kill two birds with one stone here. Take down one bad guy doing multiple things. What are the odds that a serial killer and a meth lab in the same spot are not connected?" Wyatt asked.

"I suppose it's possible," Jo said.

"Possible." Sam's face was grim. "But not likely."

CHAPTER TWELVE

Jo spent the rest of the day in a whirlwind of police activity. Between the state police, the sheriff and her deputies, and the FBI, Jo found herself fading into the background. Fine with her. She hated being in the limelight.

Somehow the White Rock Police Station had become operation central. The squad room as well as Sam's office were crammed with cops. Jo felt claustrophobic, and Major seemed to like it even less. He hid in Sam's closet. The only one who didn't seem to mind was Lucy, and that was probably because the commotion had driven Major into hiding.

She never got a chance to talk to Sam about her sister. Probably just as well; now wasn't the right time. They should be focusing on bringing justice to the girls in those graves; Jo felt selfish making it about her. She didn't want her sister's case to be a distraction. There would be plenty of time for that after.

She did, however manage to text Bridget. She had no idea if her sister was still in possession of the phone she'd given her six months ago. Her last five texts had gone unanswered, so probably not. Still, it was worth a try. If there was no reply she'd have to start a search among the homeless population. Not what she needed right now with this big case, but she was desperate to reassure herself that Bridget was at least alive.

When Jo finally arrived home at nine p.m., she was tired, hungry and drained. The site of her little cottage nestled in a grove of pine trees cheered her. She liked its remote location, no neighbors to be seen for miles. There was plenty of wildlife. Turkeys, foxes, and even the occasional deer frequented her backyard. It was peaceful. Without the hum of traffic and din of people she could even hear the brook chattering at the edge of the property from her porch.

Initially, she'd had no intention of staying in White Rock. She'd rented the cottage just as a place to sleep while she worked at the police department during the day and on her sister's case nights and weekends. But over the years she'd come to love the town and the cottage, so much so that she'd been trying to convince her elderly landlord to sell it to her.

At first she'd only intended to furnish it with the bare minimum. A bed, a kitchen table, maybe a few chairs. Little by little, she'd found herself hauling home flea market and yard sale finds and fixing them up. Now the interior of the cottage had an eclectic shabby chic feel that rivaled cottages in the decorating magazines her mother used to read.

Even the exterior was magazine-worthy: crisp white paint with red pine-tree cutout shingles. A porch ran along the front, window boxes overflowing with colorful pansies balanced the length of the porch railing. They were getting a little leggy now at the end of the season. This case was going to take up most of her free time now, but if she got a spare minute she'd pull them and plant mums that would last well into fall.

Movement at the edge of the yard caught her eye. The little orange feral cat that Jo had been feeding during the summer. The cat had appeared a few months ago, scrawny and starving. She knew it was a stray and was skittish around people. Jo had been leaving food out every day, trying to coax it onto the porch. It had let her get close a few times, but always ran back to the woods at any sudden movement or loud noise.

She hoped the cat would eventually get used to her and come inside the house. Though her lease stipulated no pets, it was getting rather lonely with just her goldfish, Finn, for company. If she was able to buy the place she'd be able to have any pet she wanted. Maybe even a dog like Lucy.

As Jo unlocked the screen door with its thick layers of green paint, she glanced at the small saucer on the porch. It was empty.

The little cat was at the bottom of the steps eyeing her cautiously.

"So you ate it all? Good kitty!"

The cat let out a soft mew. At least this one was appreciative of her handouts and didn't subject Jo to the clawing and malevolent, angry glares she got from Major at the police station.

Inside the cottage, the bubbling of the aquarium caught her attention. Finn, her goldfish, hovered at the top of the tank, his orange scales gleaming in the fluorescent light as he waited for his dinner. Earlier that summer, she'd upgraded his home from a fishbowl to a three-foot-long tank complete with gravel, plants, and a bubbling treasure chest. Finn was thriving in his new environment. She'd even been able to train him to take food from her hand.

She unscrewed the top of the yellow plastic fish flake container, pulled out a large green flake, and held it just over the surface of the water. Finn zoomed up, his lips breaching the surface of the water as he sucked the flake right out of her fingers before zooming back down under the ceramic bridge with his treasure.

"That's enough for you. Don't want you to get fat."

In the kitchen she pulled a can of cat food out of one of the cabinets and glommed some into a little saucer and placed it on the porch. Normally she would sit a bit away from the saucer, waiting for the cat to venture up, trying to get the cat used to her. But tonight she had something more important to do.

She fixed a cheese sandwich and grabbed a beer from the fridge, then sat at the vintage Formica table, barely tasting the food. Out the kitchen window, she saw the cat trotting back to the woods. It cast one longing glance back at the cottage before disappearing into the thick pines. Ideally, come winter the cat would trust her enough to at least sleep on the porch, if not inside the cabin. Jo hated to think of the little thing trying to survive the harsh New Hampshire winter outdoors.

As she watched the cat disappear her mind

returned to the case. Was the old meth lab connected to the skeletons in the shallow graves? The bog birch leaf seemed to prove that the bodies had come from somewhere near the cabin. But the question was *when?* Just because the two criminal activities were from the same location didn't mean they had happened at the same time.

They needed to find out who owned the cabin. Reese had performed a property search and discovered the owner was a trust with an obscure name— Sundown Realty Trust. Reese had connections with lots of people from the police academy. People who were free to do things that Sam and Jo might not be able to do officially without wasting time trying to get a warrant. One of those contacts was digging into the trust right now to see if he could uncover the name behind the trust.

Jo put her plate in the sink, tossed her beer bottle in the trash, and headed to the bedroom. She pulled back the corner of the rug at the foot of her bed and grabbed the skeleton key that unlocked the powder-blue armoire she used as a desk.

While most armoires held clothes, hers held notes and photos of the "unofficial" cases she was working. She swung open the doors to reveal scraps of tape and tacks. Earlier that summer photos had lined the insides of the doors. The photos had been from the Tyler Richardson case—a fallen officer whose case she and Sam had been secretly working.

The case was closed now, but she still had one thing of Tyler's tucked away: an old box that he'd hidden in a locker.

The box held mysterious photos that Tyler had taken presumably while he was performing an unofficial surveillance of Lucas Thorne. Sam and Jo had deemed it unnecessary to officially turn them in. The photos didn't show anything that could incriminate Thorne, but Sam and Jo were afraid they could be used against Tyler. They didn't want anything to mar the reputation of their dead colleague, especially since Holden Joyce had shown interest in the case. Jo wouldn't put it past him to use those photos against them somehow.

But there was something else in those photos, one in particular that had significance for Jo. She dug that photo out of the box and placed it on the vintage chenille bedspread. Then she opened the bottom drawer of the armoire, moving aside layers of faded jeans to uncover the old scrapbooks that held the notes on her sister's case.

She'd put those notes away not even a month ago, vowing to forget about the case and move on with her life. But this new case had dredged up old feelings and made her wonder if she should continue with her sister's investigation after all.

Even though she'd been led to White Rock initially with underground tips about a serial killer who had operated in the area, there was too much time between her sister's disappearance and when the girls in the shallow graves were killed for them to be related.

Decades had passed, so unless this killer had been dormant it was probably a different person.

Jo frowned at the scrapbook. Each page had paragraphs of handwritten notes, the ink now fading. The case had consumed most of her life—an unhealthy obsession? Maybe now, after having made the decision to let it go, she could pick it up again but with a better balance between working on the case and actually living her life.

She stopped at a well-worn page. It held one yellowed photo, curled at the edges. The image was of beech trees with the bottom branches stripped of bark.

The photo had come from a retired cop, Ed O'Reilly, who had been conducting his own investigation chasing after a serial killer. Ed thought this killer buried all his victims near beech trees and subtly marked the graves by stripping the bark from some of the branches on the bottom row. One of his early cases had these markings. The killer had never been caught.

No one had ever given Ed's theory merit, though, because other graves with these markings had been attributed to killers now incarcerated. Some of those killers denied guilt; a few confessed to the crimes. Ed maintained that those who confessed were either lying or taking the blame for some reason.

Jo wasn't sure why, but she believed Ed's theory. Maybe it was because the police stopped investigating her sister's case when they apprehended a suspect they thought was the culprit. That suspect denied killing anyone, but the police insisted. They had evidence that linked him to several murders of children. The case was closed, but Jo's sister's body was never found, and the evidence linking the killer to her sister was circumstantial. She wasn't convinced he was the one.

She'd been desperate to latch onto something when she'd heard Ed's story, and when her trail eventually led her to White Rock she'd searched everywhere for beech trees with those markings, but never found any— until she'd seen the photos in Tyler's box.

She picked Tyler's photo up off the bed and laid it on the page next to the one she'd gotten from Ed. The markings left by the way the bark was stripped from the branches looked exactly the same.

Why did Tyler have that photo? He had been collecting evidence against Thorne, and the other photos in the box seemed to point to Thorne's extracurricular activities as a drug distributor. But this one was simply a random photo of the woods. Had Tyler been collecting evidence against Thorne that had to do with more than selling drugs? And *where* had the photo been taken?

She logged into the police database from the laptop she kept on a shelf in the armoire. Wyatt had uploaded the photos he'd taken at the graves earlier that morning. She zoomed in on them. There were no beech trees anywhere near the site and no trees that had the lower branches stripped of their bark, like the ones in the other photos.

Her old beech tree lead had nothing to do with the killer who had dug the shallow graves they'd discovered that morning. But did the shallow graves have anything to do with her sister?

CHAPTER THIRTEEN

The station was blissfully quiet when Sam arrived early the next morning. He was the first one in, and he hoped the other cops would stick to their own stations today. The White Rock P. D. was too small to serve as a war room for a big case like this.

Not only were the feds, Staties, and sheriff's department investigating, the Colebrook Police chief—the town where the cabin was located—had an interest too. Sam had to wonder how effective the investigation would be with so many people having input, but there was nothing he could do about that.

Sam stuck his dark blue WRPD coffee mug under the spout of the Keurig, pulled an orange Gorilla Organic K-cup out of the rack, and put it in the machine. Lucy stood next to him, surveying the room, her tail swishing uncertainly.

Sam frowned at Lucy. "What's wrong?" Wait... something was wrong. His gaze drifted to the top of the filing cabinet. No cat. "You're afraid he's lying in wait to attack you?"

Lucy swished her tail.

Probably still spooked from yesterday. Sam couldn't say he blamed her. That cat had razor-sharp claws.

"Okay, let's go see where he is."

Lucy looked at him skeptically.

A quick survey of the squad room didn't reveal any cat, not even curled up under a desk. No sign in Sam's office either. Ahh, the closet. The door was cracked, and Sam pulled it all the way open. Major was curled in a plush cat bed in the corner. Sam remembered the cat had been spooked by all the commotion the day before. Someone must have put his cat bed in there. Probably Reese.

Major slit one eye open and glared at them.

Lucy poked her nose in, then backed out and nudged the door shut.

"I don't think we can lock him in there." Sam cracked the door so the cat wouldn't be trapped. Reese had put a litter box in the old storage closet. Sam wanted to make sure he could get to it.

"Morning!" Reese poked her head in Sam's office, and Lucy rushed over to be petted.

"I'm expecting a call from my contact on the land ownership for that cabin this morning. He's an intern at a law firm that specializes in trusts."

"Great. Good job."

Jo appeared in the doorway with a white bakery bag in one hand and a Styrofoam coffee cup in the other. She stopped for the really strong stuff at Brewed Awakening whenever she anticipated a long day, and Sam guessed today was going to be a long one.

Jo held up the bag. "Hey, I brought some doughnuts."

The crinkling of the bag piqued Lucy's interest, and she trotted over to sit in front of Jo and stare up at her. Lucy was trained not to beg, so she sat calmly, but she was smart enough to know that no one could resist her soulful pleading eyes. Jo pulled a tiny piece of doughnut out of the bag and tossed it to her.

Jo smiled as she watched Lucy, then her eyes flicked to something behind Sam and her smile evaporated.

Sam turned to see Major standing in the closet doorway. He gave them a bored look and then stretched, humping his back and yawning as if to show off his long sharp teeth.

"Here, kitty." Reese squatted and put her hand out toward the cat, which ignored her and walked in the other direction. "I guess I should feed you."

"What's going on?" Wyatt appeared behind Jo. She handed him the doughnut bag.

"They're still out of jelly." Her voice was thick with disappointment.

Wyatt raised a brow at Sam, then looked into the bag and pulled out a chocolate glazed before passing the bag to Sam.

"So any word on the land?" Wyatt asked with his mouth full.

"Reese is on it."

"What I don't get is why he moved the bodies? Why put them on *Frank's* land? You think the killer had a grudge?" Wyatt asked.

"Actually, it's not Frank's land. That area where the bodies were found is on conservation property," Jo said.

"Ahh ... That makes sense." Wyatt took another bite. Lucy focused her concentration on Wyatt, waiting for a crumb to fall. Judging by the way he was chowing down, crumbs were likely. "Conservation land would never be built on."

"A perfect place to stash bodies you didn't want dug up," Sam said.

Jo twisted her mouth. "But why move them in the first place? That land by the cabin is remote and swampy. I doubt anyone would build there."

"You never know. Some of the places Thorne has built on have been suspect. We know he's paying people off to get what he wants." Sam's phone dinged with a text. "That's Bev, wondering if we've got anything new on the owners of that property."

"Got it!" Reese called in from the reception area. They hurried to the squad room as Reese came around the corner with a paper in her hand. She handed it to Sam. "Traced that trust to a corporation—Mervale International."

Sam's brows shot up. "Mervale? That's Thorne's wife's family company."

Jo smiled. "The plot thickens."

"That's a great lead," Sam said. "Marnie said she was good friends with Thorne's wife. Maybe I can get some information from her."

Reese made a face. "I wouldn't put too much stock in what Marnie Wilson says." Sam frowned, wondering why, and Reese added, "Just saying she might not be all she seems."

Sam trusted Reese's judgement, yet he didn't want

to write Marnie off until she'd actually done something to make them not trust her. "She still might be better than Jamison."

"Sometimes the devil you know is better than the one you don't know," Wyatt said.

"Speaking of the devil," Jo nodded toward the window. Henley Jamison walked down the sidewalk in his charcoal designer suit, red tie flapping over his shoulder. He was headed in their direction, and he looked like a man on a mission. "Let's make sure he doesn't stay long." Sam glanced over at the filing cabinet. "Where's Major? Maybe he'll hiss at Jamison enough to make him leave."

Mew! The cat looked at them suspiciously from where he'd been lurking near his now-empty food bowl.

"Hey, kitty. Want a treat?" Reese crinkled the cat treat bag, and Major showed a little interest. She made a big show of putting treats on the top of the filing cabinet. Major hopped up, casting them a malevolent glance, before sniffing the treats as if he expected them to be laced with poison.

The door flew open, and Jamison's voice bellowed over the post office boxes. "Where is everyone? There's a big investigation going on, you know!"

"In here investigating," Sam shouted back.

Jamison came around the corner scowling. His eyes flicked to the photos on the cork board, then around the room at all of them. Apparently satisfied that they were indeed investigating, his scowl lightened.

"Can we help you?" Jo asked.

"I'm on my way to a news conference about those bodies you found. I don't have much time for chit-chat. Just stopped in to see if there was anything new I could reveal to the media. The public likes to think we are making progress."

Sam was always cautious about what to reveal to the media. It was never a good idea to reveal your findings and give the killer opportunities to cover his tracks. "There's nothing definitive. We're tracking down some leads, but don't have any answers."

"Huh. Well, this case is a big deal. The feds want in and are already out at that cabin. Have you proven the two cases are connected?"

"Not yet."

"But you think they are?"

"Yep."

"Based on a leaf?" Jamison looked skeptical.

"A rare leaf found in only a few areas in New England. The cabin site just happens to be one of those areas."

Jamison considered that and then nodded. "Sheriff's office says the bodies could be runaways that got mixed up in drugs. I suppose that would be another thread that connects them."

Jamison had been shifting position as he talked, and now he stood a few inches from the filing cabinet with his back to it. He was surprised at how adeptly Jamison connected the pieces that tied the cases together. Maybe he wasn't as dumb as he looked.

Hiss!

Major's paw shot out, his claw raking Jamison's shoulder and snagging a thread in the fabric, leaving a pull in his expensive suit.

"What the—!" Jamison spun around, and for a second Sam feared what he might do to the cat. But Jamison was full of surprises today. He stopped, his face softened, and he cautiously held out his hand for Major to sniff.

Major craned his neck forward, sniffed and then looked up at Jamison.

Mew.

Surprisingly, Jamison scratched the top of Major's head. Even more surprising, Major let him. Sam thought he might have even heard a purr.

"Nice cat." Jamison gave Major's head one last pat, picked at the pull Major had made in the shoulder of his suitcoat, and then turned back to Sam. "I gotta run. Keep me apprised of any new developments."

He turned on his heel and left them all staring after him.

"Nice kitty?" Jo's tone was incredulous.

"Who knew Jamison was a cat lover?" Wyatt asked.

"Or that Major was a mayor lover," Reese quipped.

"Maybe we should send Major over to his office as a gift. He seems to hate us," Sam said.

"No way!" Reese put her hands on her hips and addressed the cat. "Nice going, traitor. Maybe you should appreciate your cushy digs here or you might end up bunking with Jamison. I bet he won't feed you the expensive food with the gravy you like."

Major tucked his front paws underneath him and stared at Reese.

"Maybe Jamison isn't as bad as we thought, if he's an animal lover," Jo said.

"Maybe, but I know one thing: He's going to be a pain about this case until it's solved. And because that land has a direct connection to Thorne, I guess our next move is to pay a visit to the corporate offices of Mervale International."

CHAPTER FOURTEEN

The corporate offices of Mervale International were in the next town. They were housed in a long, concrete one-story building about a quarter mile down an old logging road that had been paved. The parking lot was freshly paved with sharp white lines and pockets of landscaping. Shiny metal storage buildings in the back were hidden by tall Lombardy poplars. Next to the building, perfectly-trimmed shrubs grew from a bed of bark mulch. Apparently Mervale International was doing very well.

The plate glass doors opened to a large reception area with a marble tile floor, mahogany walls, and a semicircular reception desk with a young blonde sitting behind it. She smiled as they approached, but concern flickered in her eyes when she noticed the badge on Sam's hip.

"Can I help you?" she asked tentatively.

"We'd like to speak to Robert Summers, please." In her usual efficient manner, Reese had provided Sam with information on Mervale International and its officers and Board of Directors. Thorne wasn't involved with the company, but it looked as though the CEO was his brother-in-law Robert Summers.

She pressed her lips together and looked down at something on her desk. "I'm sorry, but Mr. Summers isn't in."

Was she putting him off? He hoped they wouldn't get the runaround.

"We can wait. When will he be back?"

The girl glanced around the lobby as if she didn't know what to say. Sam was sure they didn't want the police lounging around in their upscale lobby. Finally, she said, "I'm afraid you may have a long wait. He's on an extended leave."

Interesting. Why the secrecy? Probably just the usual corporate paranoia. Whatever the reason for his extended absence, Sam doubted it had anything to do with his case.

"Then could we speak to whoever is in charge?" Sam asked.

"That would be Beryl Thorne."

Sam and Jo exchanged a glance. Beryl Thorne was second-in-command of her family's company? This provided an even greater connection between the cabin and Thorne himself.

"Then we'd like to see her," Sam said.

The receptionist picked the phone receiver off her desk, held it to her ear, and glanced at Sam. "And what should I tell her this pertains to."

"Police business."

The girl's gaze drifted to Jo, who nodded in agreement. She dialed a number and announced their presence. Sam and Jo wandered over to the large plate glass windows looking out at the parking lot. It was filled with cars. It took only a few minutes before the clicking of heels on marble announced Beryl Thorne's arrival.

She was a petite woman in her late forties. She looked young for her age, which surprised Sam, who thought being married to Thorne would be stressful enough to make his wife look like a crone. But her mink-brown hair was free of gray, and her easy smile appeared to be genuine. She stuck out her hand. "I'm Beryl Thorne. How can I help you?"

"Chief Sam Mason." Sam gestured toward Jo. "This is Sgt. Jody Harris."

They shook hands. Beryl had the strong, firm handshake of someone who had been wielding business deals for a long time.

"Perhaps we should go to your office." Sam didn't think she would want them talking about meth labs and dead bodies in the corporate lobby.

Concern flashed in her doe-brown eyes, but she simply nodded and turned. "This way, then."

Beryl's office was in the back corner of the building with a view of the forest. It was nicely decorated, all cherry wood and trendy blue-gray walls. She didn't display many personal photographs or mementos. Just a series of framed photos of owls arranged on one wall. Sam remembered Marnie Wilson telling him Beryl favored environmental causes and had taken an interest in the rare bearded owls.

Beryl gestured to two black leather chairs that sat across from her desk. "Have a seat."

She settled into the chair behind her desk. "Now what is this about? I can assure you all of our permits are in order."

"This isn't about permits. It's about a piece of land that was traced to your company."

Beryl frowned. "*Traced* to my company? What exactly does that mean? It sounds rather ominous."

"It's a property of interest in Colebrook. The deed

shows it is in a trust, and investigators have discovered that the trustee is Mervale International."

Beryl shrugged. "We own lots of land. We are a real estate development company. That hardly warrants a visit from the police."

"And having some of that land in trusts is not unusual?"

"Not at all. We have holdings for current development as well as future development. We split things up into various trusts almost like subsidiaries of the company." She slid her keyboard in front of her. "And what parcel of land is this?"

"It's out in Colebrook, was owned by the Sundown Realty Trust."

Beryl focused on the computer monitor on the corner of her desk, her fingernails clacking on the keys. She hit the return button, then sat back. "Ahh. Yes, I seem to recall that was a more recent acquisition."

Sam leaned forward in his chair. A recent acquisition? It was impossible to tell how long the meth lab had been abandoned, but John Dudley had been fairly confident those bodies had been in the ground for at least five years. If Mervale had recently acquired the land, then maybe he couldn't link it to Thorne after all. "How recent?"

Beryl chewed her bottom lip. "I think probably

within the last decade. I'm actually really not up to speed here. I've been in the background for years, but my brother's illness has forced me to take the helm." She glanced at the computer screen again, then narrowed her eyes at Sam. "Colebrook? Isn't that a little out of your jurisdiction, Chief Mason? I thought you were chief in White Rock. My husband has spoken of you. Just what is your interest in this land?"

"It's pertaining to a case in my jurisdiction." Thorne couldn't have said anything good about Sam to Beryl. Would she kick him out?

Beryl leaned back in her chair. "Then maybe I should get my attorney involved. If this has something to do with police business I might not want to say any more."

Sam wondered how many people misjudged Beryl Thorne by her petite stature and soft brown eyes. There was a steely glint inside those eyes. She was a hardened businesswoman. And she wasn't naïve. She knew she had no legal responsibility to talk to him.

Sam didn't want to have to get a search warrant. That would take time, and if Jamison was as protective of Thorne and his family as DuPont had been, he might not even get one. He needed to make Beryl think they were on the same side. The side of the victim. He had to appeal to her humanity. Even though she was married to Thorne, he hoped she still had one.

"Look. I'm not supposed to give up specifics, but your company isn't in any trouble. It's clear that land has not been used. We'd just like to get some specifics on its ownership. It could help bring closure to quite a few families that are missing loved ones."

Something flashed in Beryl's eyes. Compassion? Sam hoped so. After a few seconds she turned back to her computer. "This has something to do with the bodies found out by Frank Buckner's, doesn't it?"

Sam nodded.

"But this property is in Colebrook. What's the link?"

"There was a cabin on the property and we found evidence that might link to it what we found near Frank's," said Jo, using her soft woman-to-woman tone. Sam was glad he brought her along. She always clicked better with the women they questioned. Plus, Jo was an expert in human psychology. She was good at judging when people were lying. He knew she'd be studying Beryl to see if she knew more about the cabin or her husband than she let on.

"A cabin?" Beryl started typing again. "We don't usually buy structures, just land."

"This cabin was well hidden in the woods."

"There's no mention of any structure in the computer files. Typically we buy large parcels of land only. But there have been a few cases where someone built a cabin that wasn't officially on the records. You know those old-timers didn't want to pay the increase in property taxes."

"What is the land for if not the cabin?" Jo asked.

Beryl tapped the computer screen with a neatly trimmed but unpolished nail. Despite her perfectly tailored blue suit and high heels, Beryl Thorne was no girly-girl. "This land is for future development."

"Development? Why would you want to develop something there? It's in the middle of nowhere."

Beryl leaned back in her chair again. "It's in the middle of nowhere *now*, but we're securing it for the future. As you know, population pushes out and rural areas become more populated. We always keep an eye out for good deals." She squinted at the screen. "This lot was purchased at a *very* good price, though there's no specifics as to why. Sometimes people inherit land they have no interest in and let it go cheaply."

"So you scoop it up, then just hold onto it and build later," Jo persisted.

Beryl nodded. "We always have an eye out for land that we think will become prime properties. We buy them and hold them for future generations. For my nieces and nephews. It is a family business, after all."

"Is that similar to what your husband's company does?" Sam asked.

Beryl's eyes slid to Sam. "No. He builds commercial development in the present. He doesn't have an eye toward the future."

"Do you work for that company too? I mean, the two businesses are similar, so is it an offshoot of Mervale?" Sam asked.

Beryl laughed and shook her head. "I don't get involved in his business. I found out long ago that business and pleasure don't mix. His business is totally separate from Mervale." She turned back to the computer and continued typing. "Unfortunately, this file is incomplete. We recently changed over our computer system and not everything has been entered. I can get my assistant on it and let you know more about when the land was purchased."

"We'd really appreciate it." Sam stood, and Jo followed his lead. "Thanks for talking to us."

As they turned toward the door, Beryl said. "No problem. My pleasure." It might have been Sam's imagination, but her tone seemed to indicate that she might have gotten more out of the conversation than they had.

CHAPTER FIFTEEN

Jo watched Mervale International grow smaller in the side mirror as they drove away. "You think she's gonna be cooperative?"

"Seems that way. At least until she finds out her husband is our main suspect," Sam said.

Jo snorted and turned to look at Lucy, who was lying in the back. They'd left her in the car with the windows cracked, and she looked bored. "I can't picture her being married to Thorne. She seemed kind of nice and smart."

"Well, they do say love is blind." Sam's voice carried a tinge of irony.

Jo glanced sideways at Sam. He'd been married twice. Had he gone into those marriages blind? He didn't seem like the type of guy to be taken in easily by women, but then again he had gone to lunch with Marnie Wilson. Did Marnie have ulterior motives aside from wanting his support as chief of police?

"So you don't think she was lying to us or trying to cover for her husband?" Sam asked.

Jo's area of expertise was reading people, and she'd been looking for the signs. "I don't think so. Seemed like she was being straight with us."

The giant doughnut sign for Brewed Awakening snagged her attention. "Hey, let's hit up Brewed Awakening. I need a stronger coffee. And a doughnut."

Sam pulled up to the drive-through, and a bright-eyed teen poked her head out. "The usual, Chief Mason?"

"Please. And a plain doughnut, a maple glazed and a few jellies."

Jo pushed her blue-mirrored police-issue Oakleys on top of her head and leaned forward to look across Sam at the girl in the window. "Make that a half-dozen jellies."

The girl glanced behind her and frowned. "We're out of jelly. How about lemon or Boston cream?"

Jo let out an exasperated sigh and sat back in the seat. "Fine. Lemon then."

The girl handed over the coffees and the white bag full of doughnuts, and Sam pulled away. Jo was quiet as she opened the lid and sipped her coffee, welcoming the bitter taste.

"Is something wrong besides the lack of jelly doughnuts?" Sam asked.

Jo glanced at him out of the corner of her eye. He had his eyes on the road, and she could see the deep creases of worry at the corners of his eyes. His lightly-stubbled jaw was tight with the tension of the case.

Sam felt deeply about seeking justice, especially for families who had lost loved ones. She knew how hard he was working on this case. She didn't want to add to his burden. It wouldn't be fair to dump on him about her sister right now just so *she* could feel better. She looked back out her window. "No. Just this case."

Lucy poked her head between the seats and Jo grabbed the bag, twisting in her seat to look at the German shepherd. "Just one little crumb. These aren't good for you."

Lucy panted happily and scarfed up the minuscule fragment.

The silence in the car grew heavy. Jo needed to stop tormenting herself about whether or not she should tell Sam about her sister. She was clearly giving off vibes that something was amiss. She *would* tell him, just not now.

The police radio chirped, and Reese's voice

boomed out, surrounded by static. "Got a call out on Highland Road. Apparently Bullwinkle knocked down Mrs. Peterson's fence again. Over."

More static and then Wyatt's voice. "I'll take it. I'm in the area."

Bullwinkle was what the townspeople called any moose that happened to be in the area. Jo wasn't sure, but she thought maybe they believed there was only one moose in town. There were many moose in the area, so Jo doubted that it was the same one each time one of the animals was spotted wandering through the yards and streets.

Sam looked down at the police radio. "I guess maybe this thing really will work better than using our phones."

"If we remember to turn it on."

Sam laughed. "Good point."

He smiled at her, and Jo felt the tension between them dissipate. They'd always had an easy working relationship and trust that helped them work together. Jo was relieved that she hadn't ruined it. Despite the heavy burden of the case that lay in front of them, things were looking up.

As they neared the police station, Jo saw a familiar car that dashed her good mood.

"Crap. It's Holden Joyce." Sam voiced her thoughts.

As he parked behind Holden's Toyota 4Runner, Jo grabbed the bag and slid out of the passenger door. "Look on the bright side. Maybe he has good news."

HOLDEN JOYCE WAS WAITING for them in the squad room, but he didn't have good news.

"I hope you aren't holding anything back," he said after Sam told him about the visit to Mervale.

"Look, I want this case closed as badly as you do. Especially if it involves Lucas Thorne," Sam said.

Holden's eyes narrowed. "Lucas Thorne? You really have a bug up your ass about him, don't you? What makes you think this case has anything to do with him?"

"The cabin is owned by his wife's family company."

"That's a stretch, don't you think?"

Sam's jaw tightened. "We suspect he's a drug dealer. We found remnants of a meth lab on the property. *And* that property is tied to a relative. Doesn't sound like a stretch to me."

Holden's expression turned dubious. "That meth

lab was no longer in operation. And it's more than an hour from here. If Thorne wanted to add meth to his distribution channel he might pick someplace closer to set up shop. I just hope your zest to nail Lucas Thorne for something won't cloud your judgment."

Jo could practically feel the tension rising between the two men. Though she shared Sam's dislike of Holden Joyce, they'd solve the case much easier with cooperation. She held up the bag between them. "Doughnut?"

Holden turned to her. He was still scowling, but in his eyes she saw something softer. "Thanks."

He reached for the bag, and then she saw him do something she'd never seen him do before. He actually broke into a real smile. For some reason it put her on edge. He seemed almost as if he wanted to make friends.

Or did he? Maybe it was all an act because he knew that he could get more information from them if he befriended them. But the way he'd acted when Sam mentioned Thorne made her wonder if he was going to give him a hard time about chasing down leads to prove Thorne was involved. Was that the reason he kept insinuating himself in their cases? Was it possible Holden Joyce was on Thorne's payroll?

Holden talked around a mouthful of doughnut.

"John Dudley managed to match the dental records of one of the victims. She was identified as Arlene Cross, a runaway from Pittsburgh, Pennsylvania. But her parents hadn't heard anything from her in more than ten years. She was gone a lot longer than her body was in that grave. We were hoping they might be able to tell us what kind of clothing she had in case we find anything that matched it in the debris we found in the cabin."

"They couldn't?" Jo asked.

"Nope. She'd been gone for so many years they had no idea about her wardrobe."

"Will you be able to get any DNA from the clothing in the cabin?" Sam asked. "Maybe we'll be able to match that to DNA of the skeletal remains."

"The lab's working on that. So far it's not promising," Holden said. "I wouldn't hold out hope on pinning anything on Thorne, and I don't want to focus on him so much that we disregard other suspects. Whoever was running the meth lab is likely a different person than whoever killed those girls."

"I agree," Sam said. "But that doesn't mean I'm going to let Thorne off the hook. He could very well be involved, especially with that meth lab."

"Seems to me if he really was the drug dealer here you guys would've nailed him by now."

"Our late mayor blocked most of the search warrants we tried to get to gather evidence. And we suspect there might've been a mole somewhere in the system that got wind of our plans to catch him in the act and alerted Thorne."

Holden's eyes flicked to a desk in the corner. "You mean Richardson?"

"No. Not Richardson," Sam said. "He was a good cop. We think it might've been someone else who perhaps had access to the police department."

"Like maybe one of the other federal workers," Jo said. "Not one of us."

"You mean Dupont's killer?" Holden asked.

"Maybe. We'll never know if it was." Jo glanced at the filing cabinet where Major usually presided. The cat wasn't there, but Jo thought if only the cat could talk he'd be able to tell them if his former owner had been a mole. But how would he have known about their plans? Sure, he had occasion to be at the station a lot, but it wasn't as though they talked about covert operations in the lobby for everyone to hear.

Holden chewed his doughnut for a few seconds. "A drug dealer is one thing, a serial killer quite another. Their modus operandi usually isn't the same." He glanced at Jo. "I just hope you keep that in mind.

We don't want those victims to have to wait any longer for justice."

"Agreed." Sam said. "We have the same goal. To catch whoever did that to those girls and find out who was running the meth lab. How about we try to work together better on this one?" Sam held out his hand.

Jo nibbled the corner of her doughnut. The air was thick with tension as Holden Joyce hesitated, staring at Sam's outstretched hand for a few beats before shoving the rest of his pastry in his mouth and clasping Sam's hand. "Agreed."

Holden picked another doughnut from the bag before turning to leave. "You let me know if anything new comes up. I'll do the same." Then he looked directly at Jo and said, "It'll be nice working with you."

A funny feeling gnawed at Jo's gut as she watched him leave. What was up with that weird look? Had Sam noticed the strange undertone? It was almost as if he was trying to give her some subliminal message. But what, exactly? The last case they'd worked with him he'd wanted to make sure Jo was disciplined for a minor slip-up. So why was he acting so friendly now?

"That was weird," Sam said after they heard the door shut.

"I'll say."

"What do you think he's up to?"

"No idea. We'll just have to be cautious around him. If he's gonna share information with us, I guess it can't hurt."

"I guess you're right. *If* he actually shares everything." Sam walked over to the cork board where they'd tacked up printouts of the images Wyatt had taken at the shallow graves. He leaned his butt against the edge of Jo's desk and set his coffee cup down. "So I guess it's up to us to prove that Thorne is the perpetrator behind at least one of these crimes."

"Do you really think he had anything to do with these girls?" Jo scanned the images, her eyes coming to rest on one of the bog birch leaves lying on the blue tarp with the odd pattern of holes. Could the leaf really connect the graves to the cabin? Even if it did, they needed much more.

"I have no idea, but I don't think the other police agencies are going to put in quite as much effort in looking into Thorne as we are," Sam said.

"We need to find something to tie him to that meth lab. What about the duct tape and hoses left in the kitchen? Is that something he would use at his construction site?" Jo eyed the bottom row of photographs.

"Maybe. But they're also common construction materials. The meth lab is older. Anything purchased for his construction site would have been purchased recently, so there might not be any way to prove a connection."

"What about something in his past? If he killed those girls, he's probably exhibited some odd behavior previously. Serial killers usually ramp up." Jo knew a lot about that. In her research of serial killers she discovered all kinds of things about them, but she didn't want to go into too many details or Sam might question why she knew so much.

"Good thinking." Sam pulled out his phone and thumbed in a text. "I'll get Mick on that. We don't want to ruffle any feathers with Holden Joyce or the state police or any of the others if they think we're paying too much attention to Thorne. Problem is we might not be able to tie him to the meth lab. He usually has minions do his dirty work. But if he is the killer I'm sure he would've done that work himself."

"Maybe we should talk to Jesse. He might know something about the meth lab." Jesse Cowley was a small-time drug dealer in town Sam had been grooming as an informant. He'd made a point to catch Jesse with a little bit of pot now and then and let him go so that Jesse owed him. Now might be a good time to collect.

"Can't hurt, though he doesn't seem to know very

much about the higher-ups on the chain. I suppose any information would be good. I'll have Mick meet us at Holy Spirits tonight. We'll probably run into Jesse there."

Woof!

Lucy raised her head from where she'd been lying in a patch of sunlight and looked toward the lobby.

"What is it?" Sam asked just as the lobby door opened and they heard Harry Woolston greeting Reese. A few seconds later he came around the corner of the post office boxes wearing blue, green, and pink plaid Bermuda shorts and a pink polo shirt.

Lucy rushed to him, sniffing the hem of the shorts with suspicion. This wasn't Harry's usual type of outfit.

"What's with the get-up, Harry?" Sam was amused.

"Darn wife. Wants me to take up a hobby. Painting. Golfing. Bridge. She says hanging around at the police station is dangerous." Harry pressed his lips together. "Then again, I guess she might have a point. I did almost get shot last time."

"Yeah, your wife might be onto something. Hobbies could be good at your age," Jo said.

"Bah! Hobbies are boring." Harry bent down to pet the top of Lucy's head. "I need action!"

Lucy's tail wagging stopped abruptly, and she jerked her head toward Sam's office. Major sauntered through the partially open doorway as if he owned the place. He stopped and the two of them glared at each other for a tense second before Major continued to the filing cabinet, leaping up to the top in one fluid motion.

Achoo! Harry looked at the filing cabinet. "Are you keeping that darn thing? I'm allergic." He moved as far from the cabinet as he could get, Lucy following at his heels.

"Yes, we're keeping him, Harry!" Reese called in from the reception area.

Harry made a face. "Anyway, I just stopped by to see how you got on with Marnie Wilson."

"We got on fine." Sam sounded noncommittal.

"Well, I hope so. You know us seniors really like her for mayor, and I'm hoping you can put your support behind her."

"She seems like she's planning some good things," Sam said. "I highly doubt my support will be a deciding factor in the election."

Harry waved his hand dismissively. "Of course it will. You know the people look up to the police chief in this town. Why when I was chief —."

Fortunately, Harry's diatribe about the good old days was interrupted by his phone clanging. He dug it out of his pocket and squinted at the display. "Darn. It's the wife. I gotta run. See you guys later."

Jo bit back a smile as he turned and ran out. For all of Harry's bluster, Jo knew who really wore the pants in that family. She clearly picked out his outfits.

Sam's phone pinged. "Okay, Mick is on the case. He'll meet us at Holy Spirits tonight." He glanced up at the clock, then back at Jo. "That gives me just enough time to talk to our number-one suspect, Lucas Thorne."

CHAPTER SIXTEEN

Sam's thoughts were on Jo as he pulled into Thorne's construction site. He didn't think her odd behavior had anything to do with jelly doughnuts. Did it have something to do with his lunch with Marnie? Maybe Sam was reading too much into the way she'd been acting, but he'd worked closely with Jo for several years now, and he thought he knew all her moods. Then again, he'd never been very good at understanding women, at least according to his ex-wives.

"It's probably just nothing. I should let it go, right?" Sam asked Lucy as he let her out of the back of the Tahoe.

Lucy wagged her tail in agreement.

"Okay, good call."

The construction site was busy. Thorne was building a five-story hotel on an old farm site. It had great views of the mountains and the lake, but Sam would've rather seen it remain farmland. He couldn't wait to put Thorne out of business.

Sam headed across the dirt lot toward the construction trailer amidst the clanging of machinery and shouting of workmen. The exterior of the aluminum trailer was thick with dirt and rust, but Sam knew its shabby appearance didn't extend past the outer walls. Inside, it was about as opulent as a construction trailer could be.

Just before he got to the makeshift wooden steps, Lucy veered to the right, trotting toward the building.

"Lucy!" Sam snapped his fingers.

The dog hesitated, glanced back at him, and then swung her head back toward the construction site and continued on.

Sam shrugged and followed. If Lucy was disobeying a command he was sure she had good reason.

She stopped at the corner of the building. There was no construction going on at this end, so there was minimal risk of Lucy getting hurt. Sam scanned the piles of building materials just to make sure. Was this why Lucy had led him here? He catalogued it in his mind: rebar, lumber, concrete. No duct tape or rubber hoses as he'd seen in the cabin.

Lucy was busily sniffing the corner of the building. Sam didn't see anything there either.

But something else was odd. The ground next to the building was freshly covered, as if plans to build there had been changed. Wasn't the lobby supposed to go here? He shaded his eyes and looked toward the other end, where the construction was focused. It looked as if they'd moved the lobby area down there.

He looked behind him to the land that belonged to Jackson Pressler and was the nesting site of the Great Bearded Owls. Had Thorne moved the lobby to the other side so that the building wouldn't disturb the owls? Had it been at his wife's insistance?

Sam whistled for Lucy. "Okay, I see what you wanted me to see. Come on. We have to talk to Thorne."

Lucy tore herself away from her sniffing and trotted back to the trailer at Sam's side.

Sam opened the flimsy aluminum screen door and knocked on the hollow plywood door behind it.

"Come in." Thorne bellowed from inside.

Sam opened the door, and a cool wave of spicy aftershave wafted out. Inside, the hum of the air-conditioner in one of the windows masked the sounds of construction. The office was as plush as he remembered. Thick carpeting. Rich dark paneled walnut walls. Shelves lined with trophies. Golf, tennis, softball. Apparently Thorne had lots of leisure time.

"Shut the door. I'm not air-conditioning White Rock."

Thorne sat in a big black leather chair behind an ornate mahogany desk. The sleeves of his light blue button-down shirt were rolled up to reveal forearms that were tanned and muscular for a man of his age. Though in his late forties he still looked youthful. Probably all that golf and tennis.

"Mason. What a pleasant surprise." The sarcasm in his voice indicated it was anything but. "I hear you have a big case. Surprised you have time to visit little old me."

"I'm here following leads on a case."

Thorne leaned back in his chair, steepling his fingers over his stomach. "Really? Is that the one out by Buckner's? Surely you don't think I had anything to do with that?"

"Maybe."

Thorne laughed. "Have you been drinking? What evidence do you have to even insinuate that I would have something to do with that mess?"

"I have evidence that links those shallow graves to

a meth lab. And then I have further evidence that links you to the meth lab."

Thorne snorted. "Seriously? I'm a real estate developer. What would I want with a meth lab?"

"To increase profitability of your drug business," Sam said. Thorne was acting pretty confident that he couldn't be linked to the meth lab or the girls. Was it because he was innocent or just too cocky to believe that Sam would find solid evidence against him? Or maybe he'd paid off so many people that he figured the police would never be able to make a case without being blocked at every turn.

Thorne gestured toward the small window in the side of the trailer. "Are you kidding me? I'm pretty busy with all of this. But I'll humor you. What exactly is this evidence linking me to a meth lab?"

"The land the abandoned meth lab operated on is owned by your wife's company."

At the mention of his wife, Thorne's eyes narrowed slightly. Trouble in paradise? Sam wondered if Beryl Thorne knew more about her husband's activities than she let on. Or maybe she was just becoming aware of his drug activities. Sam doubted she would approve. If they were having marital problems and she didn't approve of his extracurricular activities, Sam might be able to get her on his side. She could provide him with valuable information against her husband.

"Then I guess you don't have much. My company has nothing to do with Mervale, so you really have no connection at all." He stood up behind his desk, and Lucy let out a low growl. His eyes flicked to the dog. "Get out and take your dog before I slap you with a harassment suit."

Sam stared at him for a few seconds. Thorne was guilty, at least of dealing drugs. Now Sam just had to prove it. "No problem. But I'll be looking at you very closely."

Sam left the wooden door open. Halfway to the Tahoe, he turned to see Thorne staring after him. He got in the vehicle wondering if he'd done the right thing.

Had he just given Thorne enough warning to cover his tracks or had he rattled him enough that he'd make a stupid mistake?

CHAPTER SEVENTEEN

Almost everyone had gone home for the night by the time Sam got back to the station. He found Jo waiting for him, seated at her desk wearing a gray T-shirt and jeans, plugging away on her laptop.

She looked up from her computer. "How did it go?"

"The usual. He denied everything."

"Big surprise there."

Lucy trotted over to say hello to Jo as Sam went into his office, talking to her through the open door as he changed his shirt. "I did discover that they moved the lobby of the hotel so it was farther from the bearded owls."

"Really? You think the wife had anything to do with that?" Jo asked.

"Possibly."

"Did you notice any rubber hosing or building materials, like we saw in that cottage?"

"No. But I didn't get to inspect the entire property." Sam came out of the office. He'd changed out of his WRPD T-shirt into plain black. People tended to avoid him in Holy Spirits when he was wearing the one with the giant white police letters on the back. "You ready?"

Jo closed the laptop and stood. "Yeah. I could use a beer."

"Me too."

Lucy whined and wagged her tail.

"Not you." Sam took her bowl out of the cupboard, filled it and put it on the floor. Lucy's attention pivoted from Sam to the food.

The food caught Major's attention too, and he started in the direction of the bowl. Lucy's bared teeth and low growl made the cat veer away quickly toward the lobby, acting as if that had been his destination the whole time.

Sam raised a brow at Jo, and she laughed. Just like old times. He'd been imagining the rift between them the whole time, just as he thought.

Holy Spirits was a decommissioned church turned into a bar. The giant oak double doors opened into a vestibule that was largely the same as it had been when the church was in operation. This fooled the occasional tourist, who then opened the inner doors, surprised to find a bar in action.

Inside, the cavernous twenty-foot-high ceilings gave it a spacious feel. The dark wooden floors were scarred and scraped with over a century of use. Giant field stones held in place by chipped mortar made up the bottom half of the walls.

Some of the original pews had been recycled as seating for long tables in the back. Round tables had been scattered throughout the rest of the interior. The bar resided where the altar had once been. The stained-glass windows above cast dim shadows of jewel-toned light into the room. Beneath the windows rows of colorful liquor bottles stood beneath a mirror that ran the length of the bar.

The favorite watering hole had a casual feeling despite its formal beginnings. Billie Hanson, the owner, kept the lights low and the beer flowing.

The bar was fairly crowded, and the chatter of patrons melded with the smell of burgers and hops.

"At least Holden Joyce isn't here," Jo said as they slid onto their usual barstools.

"Yeah, what is up with him? And what was with that weird look he gave you earlier at the station?" Sam leaned over the polished wooden surface of the bar and signaled Billie, who was serving a group of customers at the other corner of the bar. She turned and gave a slight nod, the seven diamond studs in her ears winking in the light. Her spiked hair was tipped with blue tonight. A white dishtowel was tossed over her shoulder.

"Yeah, I'm not sure what's up with him," Jo watched Billie hustle, grabbing two plates of burgers from the little opening into the kitchen and sliding them in front of two customers before opening the cooler and grabbing their usual beers—a local beer called Moosenose for Sam and a Boston Lager for Jo.

"Seems like he's up to something. Do you think he could still have a hair up his butt about Tyler's log book?"

Earlier that summer Jo had forged an entry in the log of fallen officer Tyler Richardson. She'd done it to protect Tyler, and Sam stood by that. Tyler had failed to log the call, which was against procedure but was common practice in their town. They often filled in the log when they got back to the station. Except Tyler never came back to the station. During a related investigation, Holden Joyce had found out about the log book and pressed for disciplinary action against Jo. He didn't win that battle. Maybe he was still angry about it and planning to make her pay some other way.

"Maybe. It could be something else."

They sipped their beers. The coldness of the earthy brew felt good going down. Sam turned to Jo, expecting her to explain what she thought Holden's problem could be. She silently picked at her beer label with her thumbnail.

"Something else?" he prompted.

"Well, a long time ago—"

"Hey, Sam!" a woman's voice yelled out, interrupting Jo.

Sam turned to see Marnie Wilson waving to him from across the room.

JO'S GAZE skimmed over Sam's shoulder. Marnie Wilson stood at a table, waving at Sam as if they were long-lost friends. What was she doing in a place like Holy Spirits? Trying to get the vote of the common people?

"Oh, it's Marnie. I have to go ask her something. Hold on." Sam pushed away from the bar and Jo turned back to her label, sliding her thumbnail up through the part that had become wet with condensation and watching it accordion off into a little strip.

It had seemed like the right moment to mention her sister's case, but maybe this was a sign that she shouldn't tell Sam at all. Their relationship seemed as though it was getting back to the way it had been. Why rock the boat now? Sam thought that the weird way Holden was acting had to do with the log book. Maybe he was right. Maybe it was just guilt that made her think that Holden Joyce knew about her lifelong research into serial killers.

Jo glanced up into the mirror behind the bar to see Jesse Cowley approaching. Perfect. Now she could ask him if he knew anything about that meth lab.

Jesse leaned across the bar next to her. "Hey, Officer Harris."

"Sergeant." Jo corrected.

"Yeah. Right. Sorry." Billie came to take his order. Two Bud Lights and a Moosenose.

"I'll take care of it." Jo pushed some bills across the bar and glanced at Jesse. "I have a few questions."

Jesse looked back over his shoulder nervously. He didn't like his friends to see him talking to the police. He didn't want them to think he was some kind of informant. Sam and Jo always tried to keep it light and informal, taking pains to meet in places where his friends wouldn't see them.

"What?" His voice was wary.

"You know anything about a meth lab in the area?"

"Meth? No. I don't do that stuff. I stick to pot. But I haven't heard of anyone cooking in White Rock."

"Not White Rock. Colebrook."

Jesse tapped his fingers on the bar, his eyes darting the length to see how Billie was progressing with his beers. "Colebrook? That wouldn't have anything to do with me."

"Never said it did. I'm just asking if you've heard anything."

Billie placed the beers in front of Jesse. He collected them and then stood there for a few seconds. Jo glanced over at Sam. Looked like he and Marnie were standing pretty close. Just what was it that Sam was in such a hurry to ask her about anyway?

"Okay, I have heard about meth labs in the area. I don't know exactly where, but I hear they move around."

"Do you think the people you get your pot from also distribute meth?"

"I've heard they do, but I honestly don't know any specifics. Like I said, I stick to pot."

"Know anyone who might know more?"

"No. Sorry." Jesse stepped away from the bar. "Look, I gotta run."

"Okay. Thanks."

Jo turned back to her beer. She hadn't counted on Jesse having much information anyway. They knew from previous interrogations that he didn't know much about what happened above his contact in the supply chain. Thorne had things locked down pretty tight, making sure each cog in his machine had only enough information to do their job. She guessed it was safer that way.

She hoped Sam's talk with Marnie would be more helpful.

THE LAST PERSON Sam had expected to see at Holy Spirits was Marnie Wilson. Not that he minded. It would be a great opportunity to dig up information on Beryl Thorne.

"Good to see you, Sam. I hope you've been thinking about the talk we had at lunch." Marnie had a beer bottle in one hand. Some kind of light beer. She put the bottle to her lips, but the volume didn't decrease much.

"Of course. Harry wouldn't let me *not* think about

it," Sam said. "But I don't really think anyone cares who I support."

"Not so! As you can see, we have common goals and ideas." Marnie gestured around the bar as if they now had something in common. She lowered her voice, and Sam had to lean far closer to her than was comfortable to hear what she said. "Besides, I know we will be on the same side with the Convale project."

Right. Same side. Sam wasn't exactly sure about that because she'd been so vague earlier. But he had more pressing problems. "Speaking of ecology-minded things, you mentioned you were friends with Beryl Thorne. What do you know about her company, Mervale?"

Marnie frowned. "Her family company? Not much. I know they have real estate holdings. Commercial, I think. She never talked much about it, but then her brother has been running it. She only took over because he was sick."

"Yeah, I heard."

"Why do you ask?"

"The company owns some land that came up in a case."

Marnie's frown deepened. "The skeletal remains? I thought that land was conservation land."

"It is. This was something else." Sam didn't want

to lie, but he also didn't want to give away too much. Especially to a politician. You never knew how they'd use information.

Marnie took another miniature swig of her beer. Sam glanced at the bar. Jo was talking to Jesse. Good, maybe she was getting something useful, because this conversation was getting him nowhere.

"I'm sure Mervale hasn't done anything illegal." Marnie's face filled with concern. "Beryl wouldn't stand for it. She plays by the rules. I think I told you how ecology-minded she is, right? She's not like her husband."

"You did tell me." But Sam had to wonder if Beryl really did play by the rules or was her company a convenient front that did things on the up and up so that they could use Thorne's business to bend the rules?

When he'd talked to Beryl Thorne he'd gotten the sense that she didn't know about her husband's extracurricular activities, but still Sam couldn't be sure she wasn't in on it. He couldn't imagine that Thorne could hide the fact that he was one of the biggest drug dealers in the county from his wife.

Sam had never been successful hiding anything from his wives, and Beryl seemed much sharper than either of the women he'd married.

Marnie continued, "I mean, she even got her husband to stop building near those owls. You know she goes up every Thursday morning to birdwatch and take photographs of them?"

Sam remembered the photographs in Beryl's office. Had she taken them? They were pretty good. "Did she ever mention anything about acquiring land and holding onto it as a business model?"

"Of course. That's part of what they do. Her grandfather started that company ages ago. In fact, he bought land up here in White Rock cheap as dirt about sixty years ago when the family lived down in Massachusetts. They relocated up here about thirty years ago and they're just starting to develop that land now."

"Don't you think it's odd that her family company does work similar to what her husband's company does? I mean, why not just have one company?"

Marnie scowled. "Yeah. But my guess is they financed Lucas and taught him the ropes, probably for Beryl's sake. Maybe they didn't want him involved in their company."

Now things were getting interesting. "Why wouldn't they want that?"

Marnie shrugged. "I assume the corporate positions would go to blood family members. Maybe there was no room for Thorne at the top. He can be a hard man."

Sam raised his brows, but when Marnie didn't comment further he prompted, "Yeah, families can be supportive like that. If the two of them have a good marriage, the businesses could be complementary even."

Maybe he could get a hint from Marnie about the Thornes' marital situation. If Beryl wasn't very happy with her husband, it might not be very hard to persuade her to give up information that could be used as evidence against him.

"I guess it could be." Marnie started looking around the bar. Was she looking for the next victim that she could try to persuade to vote for her, or were Sam's questions making her nervous?

"I guess it's already working if she convinced Thorne to move the focus of the construction so as not to affect the owls," Sam said.

"Let's just say she does have certain leverage over him as his wife. And it *is* her family money after all." Marnie took another swig. "So why all the questions. Is she in trouble?"

"No. Not at all. We're satisfied that Mervale has nothing to do with what we're investigating," Sam lied. "I just remembered that you knew her and thought I'd ask a few unofficial questions."

Marnie smiled but continued gazing around the room. He wasn't going to get any more information from her, so there was no sense in continuing the conversation. "Well, nice running into you."

"You too." Sam started back to the bar. Jesse was just leaving. He hoped Jo's conversation had been more enlightening.

JO WAS FINISHING her beer when Sam slid onto the barstool next to her.

"You find out anything good from Jesse?" he asked.

Jo shook her head. "Same old, same old. He doesn't know anything that's going on in the chain above him. He did say he'd heard of meth labs in the area and they moved around, but I don't think we'll get anything specific from him." Jo glanced at him from under her lashes. "What about Marnie?"

"She'd mentioned before that she was friends with Beryl Thorne. So I asked her a few questions about Mervale and the Thornes."

That's what they'd been talking about? Work stuff? For some reason Jo had thought maybe his chat with Marnie was personal. She didn't know why, but something about Marnie set her alarm off, and she didn't want to see Sam getting mixed up with her. "Why would you want to ask about that?"

"I suspect Beryl Thorne might not know exactly what her husband is up to. She didn't seem stupid, but I bet she must be starting to wonder about some of his behavior."

"Or she's in on it with him."

Sam studied her. "Do you really think so?"

Jo thought about it for a minute. "No. I actually got the impression that they might not be that close."

"Me too. That's why I was asking. I'm figuring if we can take some evidence of Thorne's activities to her, we can get her to give us something that incriminates him. I'm sure she wouldn't want her good family name to get caught up in a scandal."

Jo peeled another strip from the label. "Good point."

Mick Gervasi slid onto the barstool next to Sam. The jet black curly hair he wore just below the ears set off his ice-blue eyes. His navy blue T-shirt was tight against the muscles of his arms and chest. If Jo didn't know better, she'd peg Mick for ten years younger than his forty years. The private investigator liked to keep in shape. You never knew when you'd find yourself on the defensive.

"Hey, buddy." Mick clapped Sam on the back. The two had been friends since kindergarten, and Jo envied the relationship. She didn't have anyone she was that close to unless you counted her goldfish, Finn, and she'd only had him less than a year. Even Bridget was nearly a stranger. Jo resisted the urge to take her phone out. Bridget still hadn't replied to her text.

Billie rushed over. Mick was one of her favorite customers, and she already had a crystal tumbler filled with ice cubes in hand before Mick could order his usual whiskey on the rocks.

"I did a little research after you texted." Mick pulled out a piece of paper and unfolded it on the bar in front of them. "Do you have any new leads?"

Sam shook his head. They often used Mick to track leads that they couldn't follow through official channels. As a result, he was privy to a lot of their investigations. Because they'd been friends since kindergarten, Mick had Sam's full trust and, by extension, also Jo's.

"What did you find out?" Jo asked.

Mick turned his drink between his hands, the amber liquid swirling. "Serial killers are an interesting breed. Most of them have no remorse. And sometimes it can start young."

"Did you find anything that might indicate Thorne

could be one of these killers?" Sam asked. "I mean, he's been living here for a while and we haven't had any other killings here, unless there are more bodies we haven't found. If it is Thorne, what has he been doing all this time?"

"Sometimes they can be dormant for years and then all of a sudden they start another killing spree," Mick said. "Maybe Thorne has been dormant. He hasn't lived here his whole life, right?"

"I think he moved here when he married Beryl. Did you find anything unsettling in his background? Maybe some unsolved murders where he lived before he met Beryl?"

"No, but I'll dig into his childhood. Serial killers often manifest killing behavior when they are young. They start with torturing animals or act out in other ways." Mick said. "This was only preliminary research. Don't worry, I'll dig deeper."

"Great. See if he had any ties to the runaways. One of them has been identified. Her name was Arlene Cross. She was from Pittsburgh, Pennsylvania."

Mick wrote the name on the paper. "Let me know when they identify the others. I can cross-reference locations to see if Thorne was in any of those towns."

"Can't hurt, but if this is tied into the abandoned

cabin, my bet is that Thorne, or whoever the serial killer is, preyed on the runaways after they'd been on the street for a while," Jo said.

Sam took a swig of beer. "Probably. But no harm in checking everything. I don't dare focus on him too much through police channels. Holden Joyce is already on our case about it."

Mick made a face. "You mean that FBI guy that was such a pain before?"

"That's the one."

"He's involved in this too? Don't you think it's weird that he keeps showing up on your cases?" Mick chugged his drink, sending the ice cubes clinking together.

"I'll say." Sam's glanced in Jo's direction, making her feel uneasy.

Did he think Holden Joyce's presence had something to do with her? She doubted that. She had no link to him, so there was no reason for Sam to think so.

She sipped her beer as Mick told them what he'd learned about serial killer behavior. Jo already knew everything he told them and more, but she didn't want to show off her knowledge. She didn't want anyone to question why she'd become such an expert.

Not that she intended to hide it when it came to investigating. She'd make sure she applied everything she knew to help with the case, just not in an obvious way. Maybe she hadn't been able to use that knowledge to get justice for her sister, but she sure as hell was going to use it to get justice for the victims in the shallow graves.

CHAPTER EIGHTEEN

The little orange cat was on Jo's porch when she got home around eight that night. The sun had just set, causing the late-summer blooms to release their perfume and turning everything shades of blue and gray. The full moon peeked over the tops of the pines, crickets chirped loudly, and fireflies danced at the edge of the forest.

The cat didn't run away as she walked up the steps. It just sat there, its gaze shifting pointedly from Jo to the food bowl and then back again. Progress.

Jo crouched down, holding her hand out toward the cat. "Hi, kitty." The cat sniffed in her direction and looked at the bowl again, but kept far enough away so Jo couldn't pet it. Its orange-ringed tail swished uneasily in the air.

"Okay, I guess you're trying to send me the message that you want some food huh?"

Jo brought the dirty cat bowl inside to the sink and took out another small bowl. It was from a set of little antique dessert bowls she'd bought at a flea market. She'd thought the opalescent ringed bowls were pretty, but when would she ever use them? They were the perfect size for the cat, and she might as well put them to good use. She filled it with Fancy Feast and brought it outside to the porch, sat in the rocker and waited.

The cat approached and sniffed cautiously for a few seconds before digging in.

Jo sat for a while, letting the cat eat. She didn't want to be too aggressive. After a few minutes the cat came over, sniffed her hand, and let Jo scratch it behind the ears. It still seemed skittish, as if any sudden movement or loud noise would make it bolt.

"Good kitty. Hopefully by winter you'll at least be ready to sleep on the porch."

The cat's ears shot up seconds before Jo heard the crunch of tires coming down the road. Who was coming way out here? Sam?

The cat bolted to the woods as a black Toyota 4Runner pulled into her driveway.

Holden Joyce?

Jo stood up, warning bells going off in her head.

What was the FBI agent doing at her house? How had he even known where she lived?

Jo moved to the top of the steps as Joyce approached.

"Agent Joyce, what brings you here?" Jo snugged her hoodie around her middle. She didn't have a good feeling about this.

"I came to apologize," Holden stopped at the bottom of the steps, looking about as uneasy as Jo felt.

Apologize? Jo wasn't buying it. Holden Joyce was up to something.

"For what?"

"Seems we got off to a bad start," Holden eyed the porch as if Jo was going to invite him up. She wasn't. She snugged the hoodie tighter and waited for him to say more.

He twirled his keys on his finger, looking down at the ground. "I admit I came off a little strong on that other case. But I'd been given certain information about people in your department. Information that I now realize might have been wrong, especially after digging into your background a bit more."

He'd been digging into her background? "What, exactly, do you mean?"

"Well, let's just say that I know that your motives are probably solid. In fact, I know a little bit more about your motives than you might think." Holden looked up, and the look in his eye made her wonder if his words had some sort of veiled meaning. "Anyway, I was wrong to want you to have been punished for filling in the logbook for your fellow officer."

Well, now that was a surprise; not at all what Jo had been expecting. Her guilty conscience had her thinking that Holden Joyce knew something about her off-the-record investigation of her sister's case when, in fact, he'd come to apologize about Tyler.

"Why the change of heart? You seemed pretty gung-ho about it when we last met, and now you've come all the way out here to apologize." Jo was skeptical.

Holden gazed off into the distance. "Those girls in the shallow graves is why I'm here. We have a much better chance of solving this case and seeking justice for those victims if we work together. And, like I said, after doing my research I realized what I'd been told was wrong." Holden kicked a pebble with his black shiny FBI shoes. "And I think you bring a level of expertise to the situation that could be particularly helpful."

Holden's gaze drifted back to hers, and their eyes locked. She'd never noticed that his were brown. Hadn't looked at him closely enough. And now they were brimming with hidden meaning. But she could see that his words about the victims were sincere. Still, she had to wonder what he meant when he said she had a level of expertise.

Was it possible that Holden Joyce knew about her sister? Had he been in on her sister's case? She did the math in her head. He looked to be around 50-ish. He would've only been in his early 20s when her sister had been abducted, but it was possible he'd worked for the Bureau then.

Hadn't Bev Hatch mentioned something about a bungled case that had haunted him? Was it possible it was her sister's case? If it had, he would've connected the last names, but Harris wasn't exactly unique. But if he had, that might explain all the strange looks he'd been giving her.

"Anyway, I just wanted to come out and apologize in the hope that we can start fresh. You helped out a fellow officer and spared his family undue pain. That was the right thing to do. I hope to come together to solve this case." He gave her one last long look, then turned and got back in his car, leaving Jo staring after him.

Just as his taillights vanished, her phone pinged. She pulled it out. It was Bridget! Relief flooded through her, overshadowing her concerns about the odd conversation with Holden. The text contained two words.

Doing okay.

Jo hadn't been close with her sister in years, but she still loved her desperately. Sure, Jo had tried to help her many times. Rehab. Counseling. Taking her into her own home. But Bridget always fell back into drugs. It was frustrating, but Jo had had to make her peace with it or it would've driven her crazy.

She thumbed back a quick text.

Good to hear that. Hope things are looking up.

Jo still hoped one day Bridget would go straight. At least she was still alive.

Doing good. Staying in a halfway house now.

Jo let a reluctant seed of hope sprout. Bridget could be just telling her what she wanted to hear, but a halfway house was better than the campsites and dingy abandoned buildings her sister had lived in before. Was it possible she really was trying to clean up her act this time?

That's wonderful! Can I do anything to help?

No answer came for a few minutes. Had she pushed too far? Then another text.

Not yet. Trying to get clean this time for real. Will let you know. I heard about your case.

She had? Jo hadn't even realized her sister read

papers or was aware of anything going on outside of her little drug circle, but maybe she really was at a halfway house and getting back into society. Her heart warmed that her sister might be interested in finding out what was going on in her life.

Was it possible her sister knew anything that could help in the case? Might as well ask.

We think the victims were involved with drugs. Have you heard anything?

Jo didn't want to pump her sister for information. She was truly happy and relieved and hopeful that her sister was trying to get clean, but Bridget had opened the door by mentioning the case. Maybe it was because she knew something.

A friend of mine went missing five years ago. It always haunted me. She could be one of the bodies that you found.

Adrenalin spiked through Jo.

What was her name? What can you tell me about her?

She said her name was Amber Desrocher and she was from Ohio. Thing was, she'd hooked up with a guy from up north. Older guy. Went off with him one day and never came back.

An older guy? Thorne? She needed to talk to her sister right away.

Would you recognize him? I want to meet and talk to you. Make sure you're doing okay.

Jo didn't want her sister to think she only wanted to meet with her to talk about the case, because that wasn't true. She truly wanted to assure herself her sister was okay.

Jo stared at the phone for a few minutes, but no text came. Dammit! She'd pushed too far again. It had always been a problem trying to force things instead of letting Bridget do things in her own time.

Then, finally.

Not now. Can't see you until I make sure I'm really going to do it this time. So many failures...

Jo wasn't going to push this time. Her sister's recovery was more important than this case. If she truly was going to go straight this time it was more important than anything. But she had one tidbit of information that could be incredibly helpful. If Amber was one of the victims, and the man from up north was Thorne, and her sister could recognize him, that could break the case wide open.

CHAPTER NINETEEN

S am had a set of the crime scene photos tacked up to the cork board in his office. He ran his fingers through his hair as he studied each one, looking for a link between the shallow graves and the abandoned cabin. The two cases were related. He felt it in his gut.

Two light taps on his office door broke his concentration. He turned to see Jo standing in the doorway. "I might have a lead."

Sam spun around and gave his full attention to his sergeant. "Really? Spill."

Jo came in and stood on the other side of his desk. She had a notebook in her left hand and her number two pencil in her right. She was tapping the eraser end of the pencil on the pad in her usual nervous habit.

"I contacted my sister last night," Jo said.

Jo didn't talk about her sister much. Sam only knew that she'd gotten involved in drugs at a young age and was living in the drug community somewhere up in the area. In fact, it was one of the reasons Jo had come to White Rock.

Now the odd way Jo had been acting lately made sense. Of course, finding the skeletal remains and realizing they were linked to drugs probably terrified her. She must have been sick with worry over her sister.

"I'm sorry. I didn't even think about your sister. You must've been worried." How could he have been so insensitive? Being wrapped up in the case was no excuse. "Is she okay?"

"No need to apologize. My sister isn't your problem." Jo sat down in the guest chair, and it rocked forward because one front leg was shorter than the other. Great for throwing suspects off kilter. Not so great for guests. "She says she's trying to get clean, but who knows. Anyway, she had heard about the case and gave me the name of a young girl she befriended who disappeared right around the time the victims would've been murdered."

"Really? What's her name?" They hadn't been able to identify all the remains yet, and it had weighed heavily on Sam. He desperately wanted to bring closure to the families who were missing children.

Though considering what had happened to them, maybe it was kinder if the families just thought they were out there alive somewhere.

"Amber Desrocher. She said she was from Ohio." Jo shrugged. "Here's the kicker. She said Amber got involved with an older man from up north. She took off with the guy one day and never came back."

"Thorne?" Sam said hopefully.

Jo shrugged. "I don't know. Maybe if one of those skeletons does belong to Amber then we could bring a photo of Thorne down to see if my sister recognizes him."

"Would she do that?"

"I'm not sure. You know it's been up and down with her. She might disappear off the radar." Jo glanced down at her phone.

"I understand. Let's take it one step at a time." Sam's pulse skipped with a spark of hope. Maybe this case was coming together after all.

Another tap at the door, and Reese poked her head in. "I have some new information, and I don't think you're gonna like it."

THEY ALL FILED BACK in the squad room. Reese

had a pile of papers and her iPad in her hand. She handed the papers to Sam and talked while her fingers typed on the screen keyboard. "Medical examiner's report on the skeletal remains. John was able to determine for sure that they've been there for at least five years."

"So we need to figure out what Thorne was up to five years ago." Before discovering that Thorne was behind the drug problem in White Rock, Sam had thought he was merely a belligerent pompous asshole ruining the town with all his construction.

How long ago had that been? Sam had been more focused on figuring out how Thorne was getting permission to turn all their rural zoning into commercial than observing him for behavior that indicated he was a deranged killer. But why had Reese said he wouldn't like the results?

"What's the part I'm not gonna like?"

Reese looked up from the iPad. "Unfortunately, Mervale International didn't own that land the cabin is on five years ago. They bought it three years ago."

Sam glanced at Jo. That was a bit of a problem. But since Mervale didn't even actually know the cabin had been on that property, then maybe Thorne knew about the land ahead of time because he'd used it for his drug operation. Maybe Thorne had told Mervale about it.

"Maybe Thorne knew about that piece of land and knew there was an abandoned cabin. I mean, someone was using it to cook meth and that wasn't necessarily the owner, right?"

"Who did own it?" Jo asked.

"That's what I'm trying to find out." Reese pointed to the iPad. "I'm in contact with my friend right now. You know, the one who has access to certain legal databases. Problem is there are two kinds of trusts. One of them you can hide the actual owners, and that's the kind of trust this land was in when Mervale bought it. There's no way to find out who the actual owner of it was." Reese glanced up at Sam. "At least no *legal,* way, if you get my drift."

Sam got her drift. He didn't want to ask any more questions. Sometimes if you couldn't do things by the book it was better to not tell anyone how you gained the information.

The lobby door opened, and Reese stepped back around the post office boxes, her attention barely leaving the iPad. Sam heard Beryl Thorne's voice drift over from the lobby. "Is Chief Mason in? I have some information that he wanted."

Sam and Jo exchanged a glance. She'd come in person? She must really be worried about her company.

Sam went out to the lobby and shook her hand. She was dressed in a pale blue suit. She looked petite. Feminine. But he got the sense that she was hard as nails underneath. He didn't get the feeling that she had a hidden agenda as he did with Marnie Wilson. Seemed like Beryl Thorne was a straight shooter.

"We were just in the squad room talking over the case. Did you find out anything about the land?" Sam walked Beryl back into the squad room, and she and Jo nodded at each other.

Beryl handed Sam a stack of papers. "I had the legal department research that land. We bought it three years ago. It was in a trust. Like I said, that's pretty common."

Sam barely glanced at the papers. Reese had already discovered this, but he appreciated Beryl taking the time to come down to the station and didn't want her to think her efforts were for nothing. "Thank you. I appreciate it. Does it say who owned the trust?"

"No, our records only indicate the trust as the seller." Beryl looked around the squad room. "Do you know any more about what went on in that cabin? I mean, if whatever happened there was more than three years ago my company could hardly be held accountable."

"I don't think you'd be held accountable

anyway," Sam reassured her. He hadn't heard back from the hazmat people as to how long they thought it had been abandoned. He wasn't even certain they could tell for sure. But unless someone in Beryl's company was directly involved in cooking meth he doubted they would have any responsibility. The presence of the bog birch leaf found in the shallow graves made him certain that the cabin was directly related to the skeletal remains, but that had happened before the company had even owned the land. The question was, who was the previous owner?

"That certainly is a relief." Beryl's eyes drifted to the cork board. Her eyes widened, and she quickly jerked them away. "I wouldn't want my family name to be tarnished. But I certainly do hope you find the person who did this."

"We'll do our best."

Sam walked Beryl to the lobby and held the door as she left. Reese was still intent on her iPad. Lucy sat patiently at her feet. Major must've found a new spot to hide, because he was nowhere to be seen.

"I want you to check another person. Name is Amber Desrocher. She could be one of our victims," Sam said.

"I'm on it..." Reese's eyes drifted over Sam's shoulder, and he turned around to see Holden Joyce opening the door.

"Didn't expect to see you so soon." Sam said.

Holden shrugged. "The quicker we work this case, the quicker these families get closure. And I think we can at least agree on that."

"Fair enough," Sam said. "And in the interest of sharing information, we have a couple of new leads." Sam wasn't sure Jo would want Holden to know about her sister's drug addiction, so he simply said, "We have a name that might be one of the victims, and we also just discovered the cabin changed hands three years ago."

"Three years ago? I talked to the hazmat guys today and they think that meth lab was in operation long before that. I also talked to the medical examiner and found out that the skeletal remains have been there for five to six years. So I specifically asked the hazmat guys if they had any idea how long operations were going on in that cabin. They could tell by some of the chemical residue and the way it had changed over time that the meth lab was in operation during that time." Holden looked from Sam to Jo, who had joined them in the lobby. "So I guess that means your guy Thorne is out then, right?"

"I wouldn't say it rules him out. But it is one less tie to him," Sam admitted.

"Maybe not. What if we find out that Sundown Realty Trust was owned by Thorne," Jo asked. "It makes sense he might sell it to his wife's company."

"But Beryl would've known if he was the beneficiary of that trust. Surely she would have said something when she was here earlier."

"Wait a minute. Did you say Sundown Realty Trust?" Holden asked.

"Yes. The land was in a trust, but we don't know who the person behind it is."

"I know who it is," Holden said. "That's Joseph Menda, and right now he's in jail for murder."

CHAPTER TWENTY

"Murder?" Sam glanced over the tops of the post office boxes to the cork board in the squad room. The coincidence of a murderer owning the land tied to the skeletal remains was a great lead. But if Menda was the killer and had owned the meth lab, that meant Thorne wasn't the killer. Unless, of course, the two of them had worked together.

Holden nodded, his eyes following Sam's. "Girls. More than one."

Reese whistled. "Sounds like he could be our guy."

"Can't be." Holden's jaw was tight.

"Why not?" Reese frowned at her computer. "Says here his trial was three years ago. Our girls have been there longer than that. Maybe he just didn't get caught for these murders yet."

"I wish this case was that easy, but I don't think he could have done it." Holden squinted as if trying to force data to the front of his brain. "It's his M.O. to bury them in shallow graves, but, as I recall, he'd been in jail in Texas for almost killing his girlfriend before that, and I believe that's in the timeframe John said our girls were killed."

"That explains why Mervale got that property so cheap."

Holden nodded. "Fire sale to pay for his defense."

"I'm surprised Mervale bought the land. Beryl Thorne seemed concerned about the family name. Seems like buying land from a murderer would taint it."

"But Beryl wasn't in charge of Mervale then. Her brother was. Maybe he cares more about cheap land," Jo said.

"They might not have known it was tied to Menda," Holden said. "A realty trust hides the beneficiary's name. Lawyers could have done the deal and the officers of the company would have been none the wiser. Menda comes from money, but even money can't help when you're a sadistic killer."

"That also explains why Mervale didn't know a cabin existed. Menda probably didn't mention it so no one would discover what else he'd been up to out there."

"*If* he knew it was being used for meth," Holden pressed his lips together. "We didn't have any indication he was involved in drugs."

Sam looked at him. "No?" There might be hope to nail Thorne yet. "Maybe Menda didn't. Maybe Thorne knew about the cabin and knew no one came to the land. Figured it would be a convenient place to set up shop."

Jo snapped her fingers. "And maybe when he found out his wife's company bought it he cleared out because that was just too close of a link to him."

"Looks like we need to talk to Menda," Sam said.

Holden nodded. "He's in the New Hampshire State Prison in Concord. Best if you guys go without me... He and I don't have the best relationship. Be careful. He's smart, sneaky, and doesn't have an ounce of remorse."

CONCORD WAS ONLY A THREE-HOUR DRIVE, so Jo and Sam left right away in the Tahoe. Sam had suggested that he go with Wyatt instead of Jo, but one dagger-like glare from his sergeant told him to back off. Still, he felt protective of her as they sat on hard orange plastic chairs in the interview room, the scent of bleach and despair stinging his nostrils.

Joseph Menda shuffled in, the pant legs of his orange jumpsuit a little too long. His hands were cuffed in front of him, and his eyes sized them up, lingering on Jo a little too long.

Menda wasn't anything like Sam had expected. He was thin, wiry, with a bushy head of hair. It was his eyes that gave away what was inside. Cold and dead with not an ounce of remorse, just as Holden had said.

He plopped into the chair, a smile spreading across his face. He'd almost be handsome if it wasn't for those flat, dead eyes.

"So what can I do for ya?" His demeanor reminded Sam of a kid being let out on a field trip. He was enjoying this.

"We have a question about your old property."

"Old property?"

"Up in Colebrook. A little cabin where you might have had a side business going."

Menda's forehead wrinkled. "Don't know what you mean."

"Drugs, meth. I know you weren't arrested for that, but we found evidence on your land."

Menda raised his brows in faux innocence. "This supposed land in Colebrook? Never been there. My grandparents left me a bunch of land. It's all gone now. I'm not copping to any drug charges."

"Really? How about a few young girls that ended up in shallow graves near there?"

Menda laughed. "Trying to pin more murders on me? That happens all the time." Chains clanked as he gestured to the door. "As you can see I'm in no position to be killing young girls. Though I do wish I was."

Sam's stomach churned, but he continued. "This was five years ago. You've only been here for three."

"Sorry. Not me. They got me on all the ones I killed." He leaned forward, his eyes sparkling with interest. "But tell me, what exactly did you find?"

Sam fought the urge to leave. The man was repulsive, but he wanted answers. "Three girls. Runaways probably. Found in shallow graves. I hear that's your M.O."

"I'm hardly the first guy to stuff someone in a shallow grave. Deep graves are hard to dig or I'd have buried mine deeper."

"So you're denying any involvement with these girls?"

"I don't know, maybe if I could see a photo..." Menda leaned even closer, his breath quickening.

Sam had brought photos, but wasn't sure he should show them. The guy was practically salivating to see them. Then again, if it would get him some answers...

He took them out of his shirt pocket and slid them across the table. The shallow grave, ivory-colored bones, the hole-punctured tarp. Menda's eyes lit up.

"Look familiar?"

Menda sat back and sighed "Not really. That's not my work. Fascinating, though. Wish they had a bit more flesh on them."

"What about the holes in the tarp?"

Menda frowned and leaned forward again. "Those look like they were done on purpose. Why?"

"We were hoping you could tell us," Jo said.

Menda pivoted his attention to Jo. "Sorry, can't help you there. Maybe someone was trying to improve on my process."

"Improve?"

"Yeah, you know, copycat, but with an additional twist."

"You think this killer was a copycat?"

"Believe it or not, I have people who study me. Maybe someone was learning from me like I learned by studying the greats."

Serial killers copied one another? Sam glanced at Jo. She didn't look surprised.

"So you think whoever did this studied you?"

Menda leaned back in his chair, smug. "Sure. How does any good artist learn their craft? They study from a master."

"And you're a master," Jo said.

He tried to spread his hands, but the cuffs stopped him. He put them back in his lap. "Certainly. I get fan mail and emails all the time complimenting me, boasting and asking for tips. Of course, the prison censors them, but you can read between the lines." A smile of self-importance crossed his lips.

"Any idea who in particular might have killed these girls?" Sam tapped the photo.

Menda twisted his lips and squinted. "Five years ago, you say? No idea. I don't know who my followers are anyway, so wouldn't be any help."

Sam collected the photos and put them in his pocket.

Menda looked disappointed. His eyes met Sam's. "So if this was five years ago and you haven't caught the guy, why aren't there any fresh kills?"

"That's what I was wondering. Either the person moved on or maybe he's in prison."

"Or taking a break," Jo cut in. "Sometimes killers go dormant."

Menda licked his lips and nodded slowly. "That's

true, they do. I took a break once. Ten years." He leaned forward, his dull eyes flashing a glint of excitement. "But that urge to kill never goes away completely, so if your guy hasn't killed anyone in five years, my guess is he's itching to start up again."

CHAPTER TWENTY-ONE

"There's no guarantee the guy is even still around here," Jo said as they finished filling Reese and Wyatt in on their interview with Menda three hours later. It was after five, and both of them were off shift but had stayed to get caught up on what had happened.

They were sitting around the squad room, Lucy at Sam's feet. Major was in his spot on top of the filing cabinet watching them. All of them, with the possible exception of Major, were interested in keeping updated so they could think about the case in their off hours.

That was what Jo liked about their little police force. They were a tight group, a team, and the job wasn't something you forgot about when you went home. She'd worked city stations before and found most cops clocked out when their shift was over and didn't think about work until they came back the next day.

"He could've been caught in another state." Sam glanced at Reese. "We should get a list of all serial killers arrested in the past five years."

"Or he could be dead," Jo suggested.

"My money is still on Thorne, at least for the meth lab," Sam said.

"What did Menda say about that?"

"Claimed he didn't know about it."

"That could be true." Reese held up her iPad to show a list of addresses. "I did some research on his past addresses. He's never lived in this area." She swiped right to a document. "Then I looked into his family. The grandfather was the CEO of a big company back in the day, and they are quite wealthy. Joseph Menda was a black sheep, though. He's done a lot of bad stuff in his thirty-eight years."

Jo was impressed. Reese was becoming increasingly more competent. She might make a great detective some-day. Jo was impressed with Wyatt too. She hadn't had a chance to work much with him, but it spoke volumes that he wasn't acting put out that he'd had to handle many of the minor local calls while she and Sam worked the more interesting cases. She made a mental note to make sure they included Wyatt in their brainstorming sessions.

"I also got a list of his arrests and timeframes that he was on probation. According to the records, he was in Texas during the time our girls were killed. Unless his probation officer was lying for him, he wasn't anywhere near here," Reese said.

"So whoever killed these girls must be some kind of copycat, just like Menda suggested," Wyatt said.

"Yeah, studying the greats." Sam used air quotes around the word "greats."

The thought turned Jo's stomach. She'd heard of copycat serial killers in her years of studying them, of course, but the thought was still disturbing. Had Menda studied someone himself? It seemed likely.

But Menda couldn't have taken her sister. He was too young. Tammy was taken twenty-eight years ago when Menda would've been only a child. Maybe it had been someone he studied. Was it possible that Menda could give her the clue her own research hadn't uncovered?

"Like a disciple?" Wyatt asked.

"Thorne could be his disciple," Sam said.

"Five years ago his construction was just starting

up," Jo said. "Maybe he killed those girls, then went dormant while he focused on building his business."

"I requested copies of all the emails and letters Menda gets from the prison warden before we left," Sam said. "We might find a clue in there."

"What about Holden Joyce? He might have some additional information. I know there's bad blood, but if it helps us solve the case..." Wyatt shrugged.

"Speaking of which." Wyatt's suggestion was a perfect opportunity for Jo to tell Sam about Holden's visit, and Jo wanted to get that out in the open as soon as possible. She didn't want any more secrets. "Holden stopped by my place last night."

"He did? Why?"

"To apologize. Weird, I know, but it seems like he really wants to work together."

Reese glanced up from her iPad, her blue eyes dark with suspicion. "I think he's up to something."

"Probably. He said he got bad information before about us being on the take or something, and that's why he was so suspicious. He realized his information was false and now he wants to make friends."

"I don't know if I fully trust him, but I did think he was sincere the last time he was here. And if cooperating with him means we keep someone from being killed, I'm all for it." Sam scrubbed a hand through his hair. "Anyway, it's late and we should all get some rest. Maybe we'll find something in those emails and letters tomorrow."

"I'll tackle that job," Wyatt volunteered. "I might be able to uncover something electronically."

During the last case they'd discovered that Wyatt was pretty good with computer forensics. "That would be great. What you did with the Dupont case really helped."

Smiling at the praise, Wyatt grabbed his backpack and stood. "I'll still handle the local calls so you guys can focus on the bigger stuff."

He left, and Reese put down a bowl of cat food for Major. Lucy trotted over to investigate, but the warning glare from the cat kept her at a cautious distance.

"Are you going to feed Lucy at home, Sam?" Reese asked.

Sam nodded. Lucy went home with Sam at night. He fed her supper and breakfast at home.

"Okay. See you tomorrow." Reese left, and Jo shoved her laptop into its neoprene carrying case. She was just zipping it up when Sam's phone dinged.

"It's Mick. He says he has something interesting." Sam looked up at her. "You want to swing by my place and find out what it is?"

CHAPTER TWENTY-TWO

I f there was one place on the planet that Sam loved to be, it was his log cabin deep in the woods on the outskirts of town. He'd inherited it from his grandfather, and kept it largely decorated the way it had been when his grandparents were alive. It wasn't fancy, but it had everything Sam needed, including fond childhood memories. The furnishings were practical—overstuffed furniture, braided rugs, and a small television. The only thing that wasn't practical was his grandmother's china cabinet filled with fancy glassware and china that Sam never took out.

The warm cedar log walls were decorated with deer heads and mounted trout and bass caught by Sam's grandparents. A large moose head adorned the river rock fireplace. Sam's ex-wives had hated the place, stating that the taxidermy gave them the creeps. That didn't seem to bother Jo. She always made herself right at home, which she was doing right now by rummaging in his fridge, a disappointing endeavor because she was looking for something other than his favorite Moosenose beer.

"I knew I should have stopped at the package store and brought my own," she said, using an elk horn bottle opener to pop the top. She took a swig, then made a face. "Tastes like dirt."

Sam sipped his beer. To him it tasted like a fine blend of summer and relaxation.

"Anyone in there?" Mick's voice drifted in from the front of the house. Sam glanced over the half-height bookshelves that separated the kitchen from the living room, his gaze lingering just a second on the photo of his daughters before continuing on to see Mick peering in from the other side of the screen door.

"Come on in," Sam shouted, and then turned to Jo. "Better grab the whiskey."

Lucy greeted Mick in her usual tail-wagging manner. He crouched down to her level and ruffled her fur before standing to accept the tumbler of whiskey from Jo.

"How's it going? Anything new?" Mick asked as

they took seats around the oak mission-style coffee table.

Mick sipped his whiskey, his brows raising higher and higher as Sam filled him in on their visit to Menda at the prison. When Sam was done, Mick leaned forward, his elbows on his thighs, the glass resting between his knees.

"And there's no way Menda could have done it?"

"Nope. Reese did a full work-up. He wasn't in that area."

"That's creepier than hell that people idolize and follow serial killers," Mick said.

"No kidding."

"We also might have a lead on one of the victims," Jo said. "My sister remembers a young girl who had an older boyfriend from up north. She went with him one day and never came back."

Mick nodded thoughtfully and then said in a soft voice, "How is your sister?"

Jo shrugged and glanced down at the phone. She'd told Sam earlier there had been no further texts from Bridget.

"Says she's getting her act together." Jo's voice was casual, but Sam could tell by the way she picked at the corner of her beer bottle label that she cared deeply about her sister. She was just afraid to get her hopes up.

"If your sister's friend is one of the victims, maybe her family can tell us something," Mick suggested.

"Maybe," Jo said. "They're checking to see if she's one of the victims. We still haven't identified the other remains, so it could just be the girl took off. Runaways are like that."

Mick turned to Sam. "What about the meth lab? Anything new on that?"

"Not much back on that yet. The Staties and the FBI are still going over things," Sam said.

"And Menda claims no knowledge of that."

"Nope. Says it was family land and he's never been there."

"And you don't have any other leads?"

"None, other than the fact that the skeletal remains had that bog birch leaf, and the leaf came from the cabin, and the cabin was a meth lab." Jo blew a few corkscrew curls off her forehead, took another swig of beer, and made another face. "Maybe Holden Joyce is right and we're trying too hard to prove that Thorne is involved, and that's blinding us to other suspects or clues."

"I don't think so." Mick pulled a piece of paper from his pocket. "I did some research and came across this incident from Thorne's past. It's not public. He was a juvenile, so the records are sealed, but I have my ways."

He unfolded the paper and tossed it onto the coffee table. It was a police report.

"What's that about?" Jo asked.

"Seems that Lucas Thorne wasn't a model child. He and his friend Robert Summers were pulled in on suspicion of cat mutilation."

"Cat mutilation?"

Lucy whined and looked at them disapprovingly. Apparently she didn't like the idea of cat mutilation even though her relationship with Major was tenuous at best.

Mick made a face, "Yeah, apparently they killed a neighbor's cat and not in a nice way. Not that there is any nice way to do that."

Jo put her beer down and leaned forward, pulling the report toward her. "This is great!"

At their raised eyebrows, she grimaced. "Not that a cat got killed, that Thorne did this. This is common behavior among serial killers. They start with animals, then progress to people."

Sam appreciated that Jo had been doing her home-work on serial killers, but it was too bad they couldn't exactly use this information officially. They'd have to get some sort of a warrant to unseal the record, but how would they explain that they even knew it existed?

"So, we aren't off track," Sam said.

"No, and the timing makes sense. What if Thorne really is a disciple of Menda? If he's following in his footsteps, doesn't it make sense that he might use that old cabin on Menda's land, sort of as a tribute?"

Sam snapped his fingers. "And then when he discovered his wife's company was buying it, he had to move the bodies."

"But how would he know that land was Menda's? It was in the trust and no one knew he even owned it," Jo asked.

"Who knows with Thorne? He's got contacts and he might have been determined enough to find out. It's not impossible. After all, we did it."

"Good point."

Mick stared into his tumbler, swirling the amber liquid. "I think it's a little far-fetched that the guy is both a drug dealer and a serial killer, don't you?"

Sam glanced at Jo. Holden's words came back to him. Was he grasping? "It might be, but it might not be. At least we can check him out for both. That doesn't mean I'm going to be blind to other suspects."

Mick nodded. "I hope it is him. Putting him away

would solve a lot of problems, including a personal one for you and me."

Sam nodded. Earlier that summer, Thorne had come into possession of a knife that Mayor Dupont had been holding as leverage over Sam and Mick. Where Dupont had gotten it was anyone's guess, but the knife led to something in their past, something Sam wasn't particularly proud of, and DNA evidence on the knife could be taken the wrong way with disastrous results for Sam and Mick. But with Dupont out of the way, the knife was no longer a threat.

Sam squinted at the report. "Wait! Richard Summers. Isn't that Beryl Thorne's brother?"

Jo nodded, "The one who is sick."

"I remember Harry said that's how Beryl and Thorne met. That he was a friend of the brother."

Mick looked up from his drink. "I wonder how sick this brother is. Too sick for us to ask about Thorne? If they were that close, maybe the brother has information we could use to nail him."

"I don't know. If Beryl was taking over the company, he must be pretty ill." Sam wasn't sure he wanted to push his way in to talk to the sick brother. It could alienate Beryl.

"If he's too sick, getting access to talk to him could

be problematic. I get the impression that family protects their own," Jo said.

"True. It might not be easy to get access to him, but I know someone we can get access to, and that person might make an even more informative source."

CHAPTER TWENTY-THREE

Jackson Pressler had created an owl sanctuary on his land where the Great Bearded Owls had been discovered. Marnie Wilson had told Sam that Beryl Thorne went to the sanctuary every Thursday morning. Seeing as it was Thursday morning, Sam figured it was a great day to take Lucy for a walk in the woods. If he ran into Beryl and got a chance to talk to her alone, all the better.

If she was having doubts about her husband as Sam suspected, maybe she would open up about some of her suspicions. If Lucas Thorne was a serial killer, wouldn't he have exhibited some telling behavior? And who better to notice than someone who knew him intimately?

The crisp chill in the morning air heralded the

advent of fall. Even though it could still be steamy in the afternoons, the days were getting shorter and cooler, and while Sam hated to say goodbye to summer, he didn't mind saying goodbye to the humidity it brought.

He let Lucy out of the Tahoe and took a deep breath of pine-scented air before pulling a gray sweatshirt over his police department T-shirt and starting into the woods. This was what he loved most about White Rock, the pristine forests where you could walk alone with your thoughts and no reminder of civilization, the sounds of birds, and chipmunks and squirrels scurrying through the underbrush, the dappled sunlight dancing on the path in front of him as it filtered through the canopy of leaves above. Lucy trotted along beside him, staying back to sniff at something every so often before racing ahead to catch up.

The path was more beaten down than Sam remembered from the last time he'd been here. The owls apparently had plenty of visitors now. Good. The more awareness there was of this rare species, the more apt the public was to get on board with protecting them from the construction that was a blight on his town. Ideally, now, if he could put Thorne away, he wouldn't have to worry so much about that construction.

He almost didn't recognize Beryl without her power suit. She looked smaller, younger, more vulnerable in her maroon hoodie and faded jeans. She held a big camera in her hand, pointing it up at the tops of the trees. Sunlight glinted off her hair, highlighting natural strands of copper mixed into the chocolate brown base color.

She turned as Sam approached. Her eyes flickered with confusion, then recognition and a smile. "Chief Mason, I didn't know you were a friend of the owls."

"As a matter of fact, I am. I'm a friend of nature."

Her smile widened, and Sam felt as if he was making inroads. They had something in common, and that was the first step toward getting her on his side.

Beryl pointed to the tree tops. "One of the bearded owls is up there. They rarely come out in daylight, but sometimes they roost in the trees in the early morning. That's when I often get my best shots."

Sam shoved his hands in his pockets and looked up. The owl perched on a limb as still as a rock. The pattern in its white and gray feathers blended into the bark of the tree to make it barely distinguishable. As Sam watched, the bird lazily blinked one large round, golden eye. "I was admiring the owl photographs in your office. Did you take those?" It would have been a great line to butter her up with, but Sam was sincere.

"As a matter of fact, I did." She looked down at her camera and shrugged. "Just a little hobby. Something to get me outside."

Sam's gaze drifted in the direction of the new hotel construction. From this part of the woods he could barely see the skeleton of the building. If Thorne had continued the lobby construction on this side, the parking lot and clearing of trees for the parking lot would have made the building quite visible. "Does your husband share your love of owls and nature?"

Her expression turned guarded. "I'm not sure what you mean."

"I noticed he moved the lobby for the hotel over there." Sam tilted his chin toward the hotel. "It's further away from the sanctuary."

Beryl simply nodded.

"Was that at your request?"

She shrugged. "I may have had something to do with it. Lucas does as he pleases, usually." She aimed her camera at the tops of the trees and clicked a few shots.

Sam detected a hint of bitterness in her voice, indicating that maybe she wasn't that happy with what Lucas did. "We've made some progress in the case that involves the land we were asking you about. It could be tied to the skeletal remains we found."

Her head whipped around, her face wrinkled with concern. "What are you saying?"

"Just that the two might be connected. We don't think you had anything to do with it. Not your company, at least."

Her frown deepened. "What does that mean?"

Sam gave another half shrug. He didn't want to spell it right out and accuse Thorne because that could put her on the defensive and might have the opposite effect of what he intended. He only wanted to plant the seed to let her know they might be onto her husband and open the door for a confession if she had any doubts about him.

"It doesn't really mean anything. We have a few suspects. We think it also may be related to the drug crisis plaguing our town."

Sam watched her face carefully when he mentioned the drug crisis. Had her jaw tightened or was he imagining it because he wanted to believe that she knew something about Thorne? Or maybe it was just because he had mentioned the drug crisis. Most people got upset about that.

"You think it might be the same person? That's highly unusual, isn't it?"

"Unusual, but not impossible. We think the skeletal remains might've been runaways who got involved in drugs. Easy pickings for someone who wants to kill."

Beryl chewed her bottom lip. She was thinking about something. Sam hoped it was about inconsistencies she'd seen in her husband's behavior. Maybe she already suspected he was up to no good and this was driving the final nail home. She'd made it clear the other day that she wouldn't want her family name tarnished. He hoped she was considering the fact that her husband could be either a killer or a drug dealer, and wondering how she could turn him in without being tainted in the process.

"So you have suspects? What kind of person are you looking for?" Beryl glanced over at the construction. "I mean, I hate to think of such a person running around loose in White Rock."

"Hopefully they won't be running loose for long," Sam said. "But you know how it is. We look for inconsistencies in behavior. The deaths were about five years ago, so we're looking for someone who would have been active then. Maybe someone who had large spans of time they couldn't explain to their family. Maybe someone who missed a lot of work. You know, that sort of thing."

Beryl nodded, but her eyes had a faraway look. Sam knew he was onto something, but he didn't want to push too hard. He needed her to come to the conclusion herself.

She glanced at her watch and her eyebrows shot up. "Look at the time! I have to get to the office." She picked up her camera case and started putting the camera away. Then she turned back to Sam. "Nice talking to you, Chief Mason. I hope you find your guy." She slung the camera bag over her shoulder and started down the path.

Sam remained behind, letting her go on her own so she could process her thoughts. As he watched her disappear into the trees he couldn't help but hope that maybe the seeds he'd just planted in Beryl's mind would grow to produce a break in the case.

CHAPTER TWENTY-FOUR

Holden Joyce was already at the station when Sam and Lucy pulled in.

"Late start, chief?" Holden asked.

Lucy sniffed at Holden, glared at Major, and then trotted into Sam's office.

"Slept in." Sam ignored the pointed look from Jo. He didn't need to let Holden Joyce know what he'd been up to with Beryl Thorne. He'd fill Jo in later. "What brings you here? You have any news?"

Holden nodded. "As a matter of fact, I do. The lab was able to match pollen spores found at the cabin with spores found in the tarp that held the skeletal remains."

"So that's another link. How solid is that?"

"We still need more, but this is at least one more

spoke in the wheel, and also it's evident that there was a meth lab in that cabin. But the forensics lab couldn't say how long it's been since the cabin had been inhabited."

Sam poured water into the coffee machine, picked a mug from the rack, and held it out toward Holden, who shook his head. Sam glanced at Jo, but she already had a coffee, so he continued making his own. "Were they able to find any DNA to match the remains?"

"Unfortunately, they weren't."

"I have something that might be helpful," Jo chimed in, and they both turned to look at her. She was seated at her desk, the yellow smiley face mug steaming in front of her, a chocolate cruller on a napkin beside it. "Bev Hatch got Amber Desrocher's dental and medical records. We were able to match her to one set of remains."

Sam glanced at Jo, and she gave a subtle shake of her head. Either she hadn't heard from Bridget or hadn't convinced her to look at photos of Thorne, but Sam wasn't about to tell Holden Joyce about Jo's sister.

"I assume Amber's parents have been contacted. Did they have anything? Maybe they knew who the guy was," Sam suggested.

Jo nodded. "They have been contacted, but they couldn't give any information. They hadn't been in contact with Amber for years, which is the problem with many runaways, unfortunately."

Holden's voice turned grim. "That is what makes them so attractive to killers."

"We have another angle of attack. If the pollen spores directly connect the skeletal remains with the cabin, then we know the cabin was used as a meth lab. We need to get a search warrant for Thorne's construction sites."

Holden frowned. "I don't get the connection."

"Some of the materials used in making meth are also used on construction sites. Duct tape, rubber tubing, tarps. If we can find those same materials at Thorne's construction site, there may be some forensic investigation we can do on them to narrow down dye lots or materials and match them up. Maybe we'll get lucky and discover something that can definitively link the materials at the meth lab to Thorne."

"And what's your probable cause for the search warrant?" Holden asked.

Sam couldn't tell Holden about the cat killing because he would want to know how they had gotten access to sealed records, so he simply said, "Just a hunch."

"I don't think you're gonna be able to get a search warrant on a hunch. I have my doubts about Thorne, but I'm willing to look into any evidence we can get. That said, I think Thorne has friends in high places, and without probable cause you'll have a hard time getting a warrant." Major, who had crept to the edge of the filing cabinet while they'd been talking, let out a low growl. Sam glanced in his direction. Apparently, the cat agreed with Holden.

"I think it's worth a try. Our acting mayor is hot to get this case closed. The election is next year, and if he can close this up quickly it'll be a notch in his belt that'll work in his favor." Sam glanced at Jo. "I think we need to pay a visit and plead our case."

Holden shrugged and made a face. "Fine by me. In the meantime, we should also focus on other leads that might come to fruition."

Sam was skeptical at Holden's change of tune. All of a sudden he was cooperating, and that made Sam suspicious. Then again, maybe what Jo had said was right. Maybe Holden really was just trying to rectify the way he'd acted before so that they could work together and all do their jobs. Either way, Sam would take the cooperation. "We're doing that too. We got the correspondence sent to Joseph Menda. He thinks the killer could possibly be someone emulating him. Apparently, he gets fan mail."

Holden Joyce grimaced. "Yeah. Sick, huh?"

"Yep. But if he's right, maybe we can track that person through some of the mail he's been getting." Sam turned to Wyatt, who had been typing at his desk while half listening to the conversation. "Wyatt is looking into it."

"I'm on it right now," Wyatt said. "Had to go out on a call early this morning, but I should have something this afternoon."

"Perfect," Sam said. "In the meantime, Jo and I will go plead our case to Mayor Jamison."

THE MAYOR'S office was in the Town Hall, just down the street from the police station. The bright sun had burned off the morning chill, and Jo and Sam walked over. Once they were out in the street, Jo turned to Sam, "Where were you this morning?"

"I went up to the Bearded Owl Sanctuary. Marnie Wilson said Beryl Thorne goes there on Thursday mornings."

"You think she might be willing to go against her husband? Did you learn anything from her?" Jo didn't know much about marriage, never having been married herself, but she'd been in law enforcement long enough to witness the horrible things that spouses could do to one another. Still, a lot of them stuck together. She'd worked many domestic abuse cases in which the wives refused to press charges against the husbands, even though they were obviously mistreating them.

"She might," Sam said. "I got a sense when she came here the other day that she was protective of her family name, and I also got the feeling this morning that she might be starting to wonder about things she's seen or sensed about her husband."

"I guess if it turns out he is a serial killer, she'd want him to be in jail instead of hanging around the kitchen."

"No doubt. Anyway, it's a long shot, but we'll take what we can get." Sam glanced sideways at her. "Anything from your sister yet?"

Jo's hand instinctively went to the phone in her pocket. "Not yet. She may not even answer." Jo sighed thinking of all the other times Bridget had seemed to just fade out of existence, especially when her attempts at going sober had failed.

The Town Hall was a brick building, built in the late 1800s. Inside, the lobby floors and walls were shining white marble. The moldings, sculpted in concrete, had fancy leaves at the corners. A line of flags draped from tall posts stood beside the stairway. Gilt-framed paintings of former mayors lined the walls. Jo wasn't surprised to notice that there wasn't one of Mayor DuPont.

They took the stairs to the second floor and walked the beige carpeted hallway to the walnut-paneled mayor's reception area.

Dottie Chambers sat behind her desk, baby blue bifocals perched on her beak-like nose, eyes squinting at the computer screen. Dottie had been a fixture of the mayor's office since the 1950s, and she guarded the mayor's time like a mother bear guarding her cubs. Luckily, Sam had known Dottie since he was a little boy. She glanced up at them, her face widening into a smile when she recognized Sam.

"Sammie, you look so grown up."

Jo smirked at the nickname, but whatever got them in to see the mayor worked for her.

"Nice to see you, Dottie," Sam said.

Dottie popped up from behind the desk in a movement that belied her age. "I'll just let Mr. Jamison know you're here." She leaned toward Sam as she came around the desk and whispered, "You're in luck. No one is with him."

She tapped the thick-panel mahogany door, then opened it a crack and stuck her head in. "Chief Mason is here."

Silence ensued. Jo pictured Jamison scowling and trying to figure out how to get out of talking to them. She finally heard a resigned, "Send him in."

Jamison sat behind a walnut desk. The windows behind him provided a bird's-eye view of the rolling blue mountains in the distance. A stack of papers was piled in front of him, a pen in his hand. He looked disheveled, which aroused Jo's curiosity because she'd only ever seen him looking like a magazine model. Apparently taking over as acting mayor was much more stressful than being vice mayor.

"I hope you have good news," Jamison said.

"We may have some leads," Sam said.

"Good. I'm getting my ass kicked on this. We need to catch this guy."

Jo glanced at Sam. Jamison seemed almost human, friendly even.

"That's what I want too, but we may need a warrant," Sam said.

Jamison shrugged. "Okay. Judge Freeman is in today."

"We were thinking we might need a little bit of a push from you to help us get it."

Jamison put his pen down and frowned. "Now, why would you need that?"

"It's for Thorne Construction."

Jo wasn't sure what she'd expected. Probably for Jamison to jump up and flail his arms in outrage as Dupont used to do when they wanted a warrant to investigate anything to do with Thorne Construction. But Jamison sat back thoughtfully, his eyes drilling into Sam's. "You have probable cause?"

Another surprise. Jo hadn't realized Jamison actually knew anything about the law, much less the words "probable cause."

"We've linked the cabin with a meth lab, which links to the skeletal remains," Sam said.

"And because we suspect that Thorne is a drug dealer, that kind of gives us probable cause," Jo added.

"But you don't actually have any solid proof that links Thorne to any of these cases, do you?" Jamison asked.

Sam wiggled his hand back and forth. "Depends on what you mean by 'solid'."

Jamison scrubbed his hands over his face and sighed. "Okay. I guess it's worth a try."

He picked up the phone and called Freeman. After a short conversation that involved Jamison reminding Freeman about some Cuban cigars, he turned to them. "Okay. Get your warrant written up. Judge Freeman will sign it."

Sam didn't waste any time. He was already

halfway out the door shooting a thank-you over his shoulder.

As they spilled out into the street, power walking back to the police station, Jo turned to Sam. "That was weird. He seemed overly cooperative."

"I know," Sam said. "First Holden Joyce. Then Henley Jamison. What is the world coming to?"

CHAPTER TWENTY-FIVE

Reese set a record typing up a warrant request, and they faxed it to Judge Freeman. True to his word, he signed. Even Major seemed excited.

Sam ripped the warrant off the printer. "Wyatt, we could use a hand out there."

"Sounds good."

Sam was already halfway out the door. "Let's take two cars. Shake him up a bit. You guys can take the Crown Vic. I'll take Lucy in the Tahoe."

Jo tossed the keys to Wyatt. "You drive."

When they got into the Crown Vic, Sam's taillights were already disappearing down the street. Wyatt didn't waste any time. He seemed excited to be included, but not nervous. Jo reminded herself he was a seasoned cop, not a rookie. "So how is the search into the letters going?" she asked.

"Tedious. I mean, there's a lot to look for, and I'm going over them with a fine-toothed comb. I don't want to miss something."

"No doubt. Could be a break in the case."

Wyatt smiled. "Yeah, and I have some tricks up my sleeve to analyze the data."

"Really?"

"Let's just say I have a pretty good background in computer programming. I was a gamer as a kid," Wyatt said. "So why do you think Jamison was cooperative with this warrant? Sounded to me like he usually blocked things like this."

Was Wyatt changing the subject? Or did he just think that the details of his computer expertise would bore her? Either way, it was interesting that he'd notice that Jamison usually blocked things. Wyatt was quiet, going about his work without complaining, but he had been paying attention to the goings on at the station. That was a good sign.

"Dupont always blocked them, and it seemed like Jamison was on board with whatever DuPont did. But maybe we were wrong about him."

"Or, maybe he's up to something."

Jo looked at the rolling scenery. Wooded forest,

rolling hills, layers of mountains. Wyatt was astute in noticing the undercurrents that were going on, and probably a good judge of character if he thought Jamison was up to something. Then again, he might have been keying off of what he'd heard from Sam and Jo. But what difference did that make? The more she worked with him, the more she could see that he was a good fit with the team.

They rode the rest of the way in silence. She liked how Wyatt didn't try to engage her in small talk or start a nervous, jittery conversation. He seemed calm, level-headed, all things she liked in a fellow cop. She made a mental note to invite him along to one of her jaunts to Holy Spirits with Sam after the case was over.

The construction site was much the same as Jo remembered from the last time she'd been there, except now the location of the lobby was at the opposite end of the building. Sam was already letting Lucy out of the Tahoe when they pulled in. Lucy looked as if she wanted to run off toward the construction site.

"Stay," Sam commanded. Lucy looked disappointed, but stayed.

"I don't want her getting hurt over there," Sam said.

Thorne must have seen them pull up, because he came storming out of the trailer. "What is this?"

"We'd like to take a look around," Sam said.

Thorne's face reddened. "You can't just come here anytime you want and look around."

"Got a piece of paper that says I can." Sam handed Thorne the warrant.

The shade of Thorne's face deepened as he read the warrant. Wyatt and Jo stood silently watching. Jo used the time to scan the site looking for likely places where they might find rubber tubing, tarps and duct tape. Down in one corner was a big metal shed. She made a mental note not to forget to search inside it. The rest of the site was tidied up. The only things lying around were some metal scaffolding, lumber, and tools. She didn't see anything that would be used in the manufacture of meth.

Thorne shoved the paper back at Sam. "Fine. But you're going too far this time, Mason. I'm putting a call into the sheriff or the state police or somebody to let them know how you're harassing me."

"Good luck with that." Sam looked at Wyatt and Jo, and jerked his chin in the direction of the building. "You guys ready?"

Dust kicked up in their wake as they walked the perimeter of the project. Lucy focused her interest in one corner, and Jo wondered if maybe there was an animal buried there. Or, if Thorne really was a serial killer, might it be something worse? Down at the other end construction was in full swing. The sound of pneumatic nail guns and workmen grew louder as they made their way around the building.

When they'd made a full circuit, Jo said, "I don't see anything here, but what about that shed?" She nodded toward the metal shed.

"Yep, that looks like a likely place," Sam said.

The shed was unlocked, and the rusty door squeaked as they slid it open. It was about twenty by thirty. It was also hot as a sauna and packed with rows of metal shelving that held building supplies. Larger items leaned against the back wall.

"I'll take the far end. Jo, you take the middle, and Wyatt, you take the other end," Sam said.

They split off, and Jo walked slowly down the row, her gaze swiveling from one side to the other. Sweat dripped from under her White Rock Police Department hat. Her disappointment grew as she made her way down the row. There was nothing here but supplies. Nails, screws, brackets, and metal rods.

When she got to the end she looked at the stuff piled up in the back, but didn't see anything she recognized as familiar from the cabin. Sam and Wyatt soon joined her.

"Anything?" She asked them.

They shook their heads.

"I have a funny feeling about this. Wouldn't he at least have some duct tape or a few tarps here?" Sam said. "There was a new pallet up at the front that's shrink-wrapped, but it's all new and that won't help us."

They trudged back to the door to find Thorne leaning against it, arms crossed over his chest and a smirk on his face. "Satisfied?"

"Not really," Sam said.

Thorne spread his arms. "See? Your trip was a waste of time and your accusations are false. I'm a legitimate businessman. I have nothing to hide."

Jo glanced back and said, "Especially not when you've hidden it somewhere else."

Thorne shook his head. "Such little faith. But I'm not the one hiding things, right, Chief Mason?"

Jo didn't miss the look of pure animosity that passed between them. Thorne was referring to the knife he somehow had in his possession. He'd been using it to try to gain leverage over Sam and Mick. Jo wasn't sure exactly what the story was. She only knew that it had something to do with Sam's cousin, Gracie, who had been raped many years ago. Maybe Sam and Mick had exacted some revenge? If so, who could blame them? Gracie had been brutalized and her life had been ruined. But as far as she knew, Thorne had nothing to do with what happened to Gracie. He'd gotten the knife from Dupont.

She knew Sam wouldn't let the threat stop him from prosecuting Thorne. She doubted the threat had much power, anyway, because Sam couldn't have done anything really bad. He was too good a person.

"I get your drift, Thorne," Sam said. "Where are your smaller supplies? Hoses, duct tape, that sort of thing?"

"We use that up real quick. I have a new shipment over there." Thorne pointed to a shrink-wrapped pallet at the beginning of the aisle that Sam had inspected. It wouldn't help them in this case. They needed to find something that had been lying around for five years. Something they could use to compare with the items found in the cabin.

"I bet you do," Sam said.

"I don't know what you're after, but I haven't done anything wrong, and now that you didn't find what you were looking for you can stop harassing me." Thorne took a step closer to Sam, but Lucy's low growl had him quickly backing up. "I don't think you want to find out how it feels to be accused of something."

The tension grew as Sam and Thorne stared at each other. Then Sam turned and walked back to the Tahoe without another word. Lucy followed, casting one threatening glare back at Thorne. Jo and Wyatt brought up the rear.

"What was that about?" Wyatt asked as they got into the Crown Vic.

"Typical Thorne." Jo glanced sideways at Wyatt. Would he press her to find out what Thorne's threat was about? But to his credit, he didn't. He simply started the car and drove.

"Maybe that's why Jamison was so cooperative. He knew he was going to tip Thorne off, anyway," Wyatt said.

"That could very well be." Jo settled back into her seat. She liked where Wyatt was coming from, his thought process. But it made her wonder. Was Jamison in on things with Thorne and pretending to play both sides? If so, he might be an even craftier foe than Dupont had been.

IT WAS ALMOST five in the afternoon when they

returned to the station. They pulled their chairs in a circle in the squad room. Lucy sat beside Sam, Major skulked around the perimeter of the circle behind them, weaving his way around the back legs of their chairs while casting wary glances at Lucy. He took care to stay far enough away so no one could reach down and pet him. At least he'd come down from his supervisory post atop the filing cabinet.

"You didn't even find one thing?" Reese glanced behind her at the photos on the cork board. "Not even any remnants of old tarps?"

"No, which is suspicious in itself because you usually find tarps at a construction site," Sam said.

"Looks like he got rid of things," Wyatt said.

"So someone tipped him off?" Reese asked.

Sam nodded. "But who?"

"Jamison?" Wyatt asked.

"Or his wife," Sam said. "Maybe I shouldn't have dropped so many hints to her. I was hoping we could get her to volunteer some information."

"I think you did the right thing," Wyatt said. "I mean, who wants to be married to a serial killer? If you were, you'd think you'd want him put away pretty quick."

Jo looked into the bakery bag that sat on the corner of her desk. Even the promise of a jelly doughnut didn't lift her spirits. Good thing, because the bag held only chocolate glazed. Probably for the best. She needed to cut back on her sweets consumption. Wyatt stood and rolled his chair back behind his desk. "We still have those letters from Menda's disciples. We might find something useful in there."

"Did you find anything interesting so far?" Sam asked.

Wyatt shook his head. "They're mostly cryptic and vague references, and most of them are emails. So there's very few physical return addresses to follow up on. A couple of them went to post office boxes so I'm trying to get the records of who the owners were. One went to a real address, but that guy died six years ago so he's probably not our guy."

Jo checked her phone for the millionth time. No text from Bridget. Worry about her sister battled with her desire to get a new lead. Even if Bridget had seen the boyfriend, that had been five years ago and memories got fuzzy. Then there was the question of her drug history. Not only would she quickly be discredited in court, but could they really trust her memory to be accurate?

"Anything from your sister?" The concern on Sam's face showed that he could sense her worry.

Jo gave him a wan smile. "No."

"It would be helpful if she could describe the boyfriend, but that's not critical. Her testimony would likely be questioned, given her history. So it's more important that she get better than we pester her to help on the case," Sam said.

"Thank you." Jo knew that Sam's worry was sincere, and it warmed her heart.

The lobby door opened, and they heard Bev's voice a few seconds before she walked around the post office boxes and into the squad room. It took Jo a second to recognize her because she wasn't wearing her sheriff uniform. Tonight she had on a T-shirt, jean jacket, and jeans. Jo bit back a smile. She'd never pictured that Bev had anything in her wardrobe other than those brown and tan uniforms. She looked like she was ready for a night out at Holy Spirits. Jo mentally added her to her list of invitees.

"You folks are working late. Did you get a lead?" Bev asked.

"We wish. We're just reviewing what we have so far," Sam said. "We could use a good lead, if you have one."

"Unfortunately I don't." Bev leaned her hip on one of the desks. "Turns out those meth people were smart. No fingerprints in the kitchen. The main house had a variety of them, but nothing in AFIS, so we can't track down who they belong to." Bev rattled off the details with her usual efficiency.

"So the prints are probably from people other than those running the meth lab?" Reese asked. "Unless, of course, the people running it had never been arrested."

Bev nodded. "Possibly the drug addicts that hung out there. It's also possible the meth lab was in operation at a different time than when the vagrants squatted there. They may not even be related."

"Looks like we have a lot of things that may or may not be related," Sam said.

Bev nodded, "And so far very few solid leads."

"Anyone heard from Holden? He might have some new information," Jo said hopefully.

Bev rolled her eyes, "Yeah, I heard from him. He doesn't have anything. You know, sometimes I think those feds just butt in when they don't have anything of their own to go on. Then they take the credit for all of our work."

Jo smiled. She knew there was no love lost between Bev and Holden Joyce. In fact, she guessed he'd done exactly that to her in the past, but now that Holden seemed to be cooperating she hoped things would be different.

Sam had walked over to the cork board and was staring at the photos again. Jo knew his process was to mull over the physical clues. She was more about the psychology of suspects, but in this case there wasn't much psychology to analyze. She was going to rely mostly on Sam.

"There's got to be something in these photos that we can use," Sam glanced at his phone. "It's past five. Maybe we should all head home. I don't know about you guys, but I could use a fresh night's sleep. Maybe something will pop out at me tomorrow. Sooner or later, something's got to break."

CHAPTER TWENTY-SIX

Sam spent a restless night, his brain working overtime to make sense of the clues. He was worried about Thorne's threat, not so much for himself, but for Mick. He didn't want his friend to be pulled into some trumped-up investigation with fake evidence, but there was nothing he could do about that right now. He certainly wasn't going to throw the investigation over it. Once Thorne was gone, that threat would be gone too, so the sooner they could nail Thorne on at least one of these cases the better.

But something was bothering him, niggling away at the back of his brain like an itch that no amount of scratching would satisfy. There was also the fact that only two girls had been identified. Two families at least had closure, but one family was still wondering, and Sam desperately wanted to be able to stop that agonizing feeling of not knowing for them. Sam thought about his twin daughters, Hayley and Marla. He couldn't imagine what it would feel like if one of them disappeared from his life.

He got to the station about an hour early, surprised to find Wyatt already there. He stopped at Wyatt's desk before heading to the sanctuary of his office. "How's it going?"

Wyatt looked up from the computer, his eyes blurry. Had the guy been at this all night? "Tedious, but I'm checking everything. I'm getting into the IP layer now to see where these emails came from, and I have a special program that's going to ferret out any consistencies. It's a long shot, but..."

Sam nodded. In his limited knowledge of computers, he knew the IP layer was the technical way computers communicated with each other. Luckily, he didn't have to know any more than that. Wyatt was an expert, and that was good enough for him.

"Woof!"

"Hiss!"

Major darted out of Sam's office and shot under Kevin's desk.

Wyatt's brows crept up. "Looks like the morning is off to a great start with those two."

Sam left Wyatt to his task. In his office he found Lucy lying in a puddle of sunlight below the windows, her eye on the door, probably watching to make sure Major didn't try to intrude into her territory again. Sam went over and patted the top of her head. "You showed him, huh?"

Lucy's tail swished on the floor in agreement.

Sam got busy staring at the photos on his cork board again. Was his desperation to arrest Thorne messing with his head? So far, he'd spent all this time trying to figure out how to get evidence against Thorne in both cases, but what if the two cases were unrelated?

He should spend some time thinking about that, but he had no other suspects. He felt strongly that Thorne at least had something to do with the meth lab. The coincidences were just too much. But the murders? Maybe he had been stretching it. Thoughts of his girls surfaced again. He owed it to the families to make sure he approached this case the right way, without prejudice, so that they could catch the killer. He still remembered Menda's parting words about how the killer must be itching to start up again.

"Deep in thought, huh?"

Harry Woolston stood in Sam's doorway, dressed

in white shorts, a white shirt and terrycloth bands on his wrists and forehead.

Sam was too busy taking in Harry's outfit to formulate words.

"I know that look," Harry said. "That's when you're stuck on the case. Maybe you need to call me in?"

"I don't know, Harry. Looks like you're kind of busy."

Harry ignored his remark. "What's the problem? You may need to think outside the lines. That's what I always had to do."

"Yeah. I can see with that outfit." Sam gestured up and down Harry's body.

Harry rolled his eyes. "Tennis. The wife has me trying out all these new things." Harry sighed. "I'd rather be doing detective work. Don't you need a consultant? I have lots of experience."

"Yeah. Maybe we could use you to go undercover at the country club," Sam joked.

"Very funny. Anyway, let me tell you about a similar case I had back in my day..."

As Harry droned on about his case, Sam let his mind wander. There had to be a clue he was missing, and he had to figure it out fast because the more time that went by the better the chance the killer would strike again.

WYATT LOOKED up from his computer only long enough to see Harry Woolston disappear into Sam's office. He liked the old guy's tenacity. It reminded him of his grandfather. They had been close when Wyatt was little, but Wyatt didn't have many memories of him because circumstances had forced him and his mother to leave town when he was barely ten. He'd never seen his grandfather again, but that was probably for the best.

He dragged his attention back to the computer, not wanting to dredge up painful memories. He really hoped he could help with the case. It would make him feel as if he were atoning. How much atonement he would need, he had no idea. Would he ever feel that he'd set things right? At least he was starting to like Sam and Jo. They were honest, and he really felt they wanted to work for justice, just like him.

But what was that comment Thorne had made when they'd been at the construction site? Clearly, there was something going on between him and Sam. Wyatt couldn't imagine what it was. He'd come across people like Thorne before. The guy was bad news. So, if he was threatening to blackmail Sam with something, that only moved Sam higher in Wyatt's estimation.

Wyatt zoned out. Watching the green numbers scroll on his screen, he let the program he'd written do the work. When he and his mother had broken off contact with the family, Wyatt had been lonely. He turned to video games and computers. He'd became somewhat of an expert, and that expertise was coming in handy right now. Last night, he'd written a program to look for consistencies in the correspondence sent to Joseph Menda.

He knew from reading the letters that the correspondents didn't come right out and talk about killing. They were smart enough to know that police read each word. Instead, the real meanings were cleverly disguised behind code words. Some talked about his clever "art." Others about his masterful "accomplishments." One guy even used landscaping jargon that was clearly euphemisms for killing. It was crazy the different ways they could come up with to hide what they were really trying to say.

They weren't all serial killers, of course. Most of them were fantasizing about killing and would never escalate to the real thing. Of course, most of the letters and emails weren't signed or used nicknames.

Wyatt's program was written to key off certain phrases that he'd determined would signal someone who was serious, as well as ferret out letters that appeared to be from the same person and where at least one had been sent fairly recently. Wyatt figured that if the killer was trying to impress Menda, he'd have written him a few times, and if he was still alive he might have sent one not that long ago.

His eyes shifted from the screen to Major, who was skulking around the perimeter of the room, stopping to sniff here and there every once in a while, looking up at him as if they had some sort of special bond. Maybe they did. They were both new to the station, and both feeling their way out, trying to find acceptance, figuring out where they belonged.

Ding!

His attention jerked back to the screen. The computer had found commonalities in a five-year-old email with one that had been sent three weeks ago. The emails were unsigned and sent from different places, but they had to be from the same person. Both referred to baking, of all things, and Wyatt's blood chilled as he saw that the latest one referred to an irresistible craving to bake his favorite pie again soon.

He got to work typing furiously, trying to find the source of the email. He was working so hard he didn't notice that Jo had come in until she was standing right beside his desk looking down at the screen, a furrow between her gray eyes. "Did you find something?"

Wyatt looked up at her, excitement building in his veins. "I did. I found a common thread between some old emails and some new ones. I think this could be our guy, and even better"——he pointed to the screen —"I have an IP address, and I've traced it to a cyber café near here."

Jo leaned in even closer. "Where?"

"Black Cat Café. On Grove Street."

Jo's frown deepened. "Grove Street is right near the Summers' mansion. Thorne's in-laws."

CHAPTER TWENTY-SEVEN

The Black Cat Café was about ten minutes away in a little area of shops that had sprung up on a well-traveled road. It wasn't hard to spot, given that it had an oversized sign that depicted a giant black cat lounging along the top. The cat reminded Jo of Major, and she half expected the place to have a resident gang of cats inside. She was disappointed to discover otherwise.

The interior was what she would have described as urban trendy, a little progressive for their rural area. It was steeped in the earthy smell of coffee and buzzing with activity. People sat around in comfy micro suede purple and blue chairs, sipping steaming cappuccinos. The foam, no doubt, artistically swirled in the image of a cat. Others nibbled scones and picked cinnamon-topped pieces of coffee cake at round bistro tables.

Near the windows in the corner, a long bar-height table held three computer stations. A piece of paper hung above with instructions on how to access the Internet. While the rest of the café was uber modern, this part was like a throwback to pre-wi-fi days when it was a big draw for a café to offer computers you could use to get online. Jo hardly ever saw that anywhere anymore now that everyone had their own laptops and wi-fi was everywhere. Maybe the Internet was spotty here.

They headed to the register, passing a case loaded with fancy pastries. Sam flashed a piece of paper with a photo of Thorne at the cashier, a twenty-something with a long, blond braid pulled over one shoulder. "Does this guy come in?"

She squinted at the photo, then looked back at Sam. "I'm not sure. I don't think so."

"Maybe he uses the computers?" Sam gestured toward the computers in the corner.

The girl looked at the photo again and frowned. "Hardly anyone uses those. Gary, the owner, only has them for those of us less fortunate. He likes to help people who are not as privileged as we are," she said proudly.

"So you can't say whether this guy comes in or not?" Sam asked.

"I can't say for sure." She glanced around the room. "It's so busy in here. Everyone kind of blends in unless they're a regular. This guy is not a regular, but I only work mornings."

"Is there someone else here we could talk to? Maybe someone else saw him." Sam said.

"Sure." She glanced at another twenty-something, this one a tall guy with shaggy hair. "Hey, Matt. This guy has a question. Wants to know if you recognize a customer."

Matt shambled over and looked at the photo, then shook his head. "Did this guy do something?"

"No," Sam said, "We're just trying to locate him."

Matt looked as if he didn't quite believe Sam, but he shrugged and said, "I don't remember seeing him. He might have come in when I wasn't working."

"He would have been using the computers over there." Sam jerked his head toward the computers. "Do those get much use?"

"A few times a week, sometimes more. Depends. It's free so people who can't afford the Internet or a computer come in to use them when they want to get online."

Or, if they don't want their online activities tracked, Jo thought.

"And are you here all the time?" Sam asked.

Matt shook his head. "I work most days in the summer, but only weekends once college starts."

"Can I get a list of the other employees?" Sam asked.

A worried look passed over Matt's face, and he glanced at the girl with the braid. "I'm not sure. Maybe you should talk to our boss, Gary." He opened a drawer and reached in and pulled out a business card, which he handed to Sam.

"Thanks." Sam turned away from the counter, disappointment evident on his face. "When was that last email sent?"

"Two weeks ago," Wyatt said.

"Maybe we need to set up surveillance outside the café." Sam said. "I wonder if Bev Hatch has anyone she could spare. If Thorne comes back in and we can get a photo of him using the computer, then match that with the time the email was sent, it could go a long way to improving our case."

"And if he's starting up again. As the last email might indicate, he probably will come in to brag some more," Wyatt said.

The door opened, and Beryl Thorne walked in,

stopping short when she saw them standing there. The photo of Thorne crinkled as Sam shoved it in his pocket.

"Chief Mason." Her curious gaze darted from Sam to Jo, and then to Wyatt. Then a frown formed between her brows. "What brings you here?"

"Just following a lead," Sam said.

Beryl looked around the room and leaned in, lowering her voice. "You mean on what you found in the woods?" Her voice held a note of incredulity, as if she couldn't figure out what the café could have to do with skeletal remains.

Normally Sam would never reveal that he was following a lead. He didn't like to give out too much information, but Jo knew he was trying to make Beryl nervous, get her uncomfortable enough to give them some evidence against her husband. If she knew that Thorne came here to use the computers, the fact that the police were snooping around might be the very thing that finally caused her to realize that her suspicions about her husband really did have merit.

"Here?" She glanced around the café.

"Not anyone in here right now," Sam said. "What are you doing here?"

Her gaze darted to the pastry case. "Oh, I'm on my way to visit my brother. He doesn't get out very much these days, and he loves the cream horns here, so I always bring him some."

"Does your family come here often?" Sam asked.

The crease between her brows deepened. "No. I mean, we used to, but... Why do you ask? I thought you said Mervale wasn't connected to anything you found."

"Mervale isn't," Sam said. The slight emphasis he put on the word "Mervale" was barely noticeable, but if Beryl was already thinking her husband might be involved, it could be a subtle hint.

She nibbled her bottom lip. "Well, I want to help, if I can. If you could be more specific about what you're looking for here, maybe I've seen something on the occasions I've been here."

"We're looking for someone who might have been using the computers."

Beryl glanced over at the computers and back at Sam. "For what?"

"I'm really not at liberty to say, but some sort of communication they might not want anyone to know about. You haven't noticed anyone strange using them when you've been here?"

Beryl shook her head. "No, I never notice who is over there." But the way she glanced at the computers again told Jo that she wasn't as confident as her words sounded.

"Yeah, it was a long shot," Sam said. "Well, have a nice day."

Jo and Wyatt followed Sam to the door. As they spilled out onto the sidewalk, Jo glanced back in the shop to see Beryl Thorne staring after them, a look of worry on her face.

JO SLID her sunglasses down over her eyes and settled into the back of the Tahoe, letting Wyatt and Sam ride in the front. She glanced at the empty seat beside her, where Lucy would normally sit. They'd left the dog back at the station, figuring they couldn't bring her into the café anyway, and she'd be more comfortable in her own dog bed than sitting in the hot car. Lucy hadn't seemed to agree at the time, but Jo was willing to bet Reese had made the offer more appealing by feeding her treats.

"We need to find something to tie Thorne to those emails," Jo said, as she watched the shops give way to wooded areas and fields. In the distance, the blue waters of the lake sparkled in a basin ringed by a wall of hazy blue mountains. If Thorne had his way, most of the scenery would be replaced with condos, hotels, and strip malls in the not-so-distant future.

"If he actually is the one who sent them," Sam said.

Jo shifted her gaze from the window to meet Sam's eyes in the rear-view mirror. "You're having doubts that was him?"

"I just wanted to make sure we don't overlook someone else because we're so hot to pin it on Thorne."

"I think you've been talking to Holden Joyce too much," Jo said.

Sam snorted. "No, but he is right about not focusing too much on one person so that you don't even look at other suspects."

"It would be convenient if it was Thorne, though," Wyatt added.

"True, but we want to make sure we get the right guy. We don't want to let a serial killer go free," Sam said.

"Or a meth manufacturer." Jo glanced at her phone. Still no text from Bridget. "We need to show his photo around to the other people who work there," Jo said.

"I've got the manager's card. I'll get Reese right on it," Sam said.

"Good luck with that. I get the impression that people there all look the same to those kids," Jo replied.

"I think the wife is a little nervous." Wyatt's gaze was fixed out the side window. Jo wondered if he was watching the scenery and wondering what the future might hold, as she was.

"Maybe we got her thinking," Sam said.

"I wonder if Thorne told her we searched the construction site," Jo said.

"It might be good if he did. That would give her some more to think about. I'm hoping that over time she'll realize it's not going to benefit her to cover up for him." Sam glanced in the rearview mirror at Jo. "What do you think, Jo? Human behavior is more your department than mine."

Jo had been watching Beryl Thorne. The telltale signs of nervousness were there, no doubt, but she couldn't tell whether it was because Beryl knew something about Thorne or simply because their paths kept crossing in relation to the case.

Even if Thorne wasn't the killer, he sure as hell was one of the biggest drug distributors in the area, and his wife had to have some inkling about that. "I think Beryl knows something. She had a nervous twitch, and her eyes were darting around the café, but I'm not sure she knows anything concrete. It could be something subconscious. You know, like she knows something is off but doesn't want to admit to herself that her husband could be involved in something shady."

"She definitely seemed worried," Wyatt said. "I only wish we had something more than just a hope that she might rat out her husband."

"If we just had a better way of knowing who was at the computer at the time the email was sent," Sam glanced at Wyatt. "You don't have any computer tricks for that, I suppose."

"I wish. I can only trace the email to a specific computer using the IP layer and decoding the MAC address, but that won't help us because anyone could have sat at that computer during the time. And who's going to remember who was there a couple of weeks ago?"

"Maybe they have surveillance cameras," Jo asked, hopefully.

Sam shook his head. "I didn't see any in there."

If Sam said there weren't any surveillance cameras, you could bet money on it. Sam had a knack for noticing those kinds of details.

"If this was the city, we could pull up traffic camera footage and we might be able to catch him going into the café, or if we're lucky, one of the cameras might actually show the café window," Wyatt said. "But of course, we don't have traffic cameras here."

"Yeah. One of the disadvantages of working in a small town, I suppose," Jo said.

"Yep, but I wouldn't want to live anywhere else." Sam glanced out the window, and Jo followed his gaze. The uncluttered scenery had given way to the beginnings of Main Street. What once had been a large farm where sheep and cattle had grazed, a new strip mall had been built. Jo's chest constricted. How soon before their idyllic small-town life became just like city life?

Judging by the pace they were putting up that strip mall—one of Thorne's—it would seem pretty soon. The grazing field had been replaced with blacktop. Where stands of pines and oaks once stood now was a concrete block building, its plate glass windows reflecting glare from the sun. The only saving grace was that Thorne had put a large landscaped area at the end of the parking lot beside the road, and several spots in the parking lot had been landscaped with shrubs and flowers.

Jo had to admit the landscaping was kind of nice. They'd planted hostas, colorful flowers, and trees. Grass was starting to sprout in the ten-foot-wide area separating the parking lot and the road. Thorne was even putting in an irrigation system. One of the kids who worked for him was going over the hard-packed ground with an aeration machine to prep for it. The landscaped area was one of the concessions Thorne had had to make to get the zoning board to agree to rezone this parcel for commercial use.

As they pulled down the street, a familiar black Toyota 4Runner was parked in front of the police station. "Looks like the FBI is here," Jo announced. "Maybe there's been a break in the case."

CHAPTER TWENTY-EIGHT

Sam followed Jo and Wyatt into the police station. Reese looked up from her desk, rolled her eyes, and tilted her head toward the squad room where Holden Joyce sat in a chair feeding treats to Lucy and getting the stink eye from Major, perched in his usual place on top of the filing cabinet.

Sam handed Reese the card he'd gotten from the café. "Can you call this guy? He's the owner of the café, and I want to get the names of all his employees and the times they work so we can go down and show them Thorne's photo."

Lucy met him as they came around the post office boxes. She was clearly relieved that Sam and Jo were back, and that Holden wasn't going to be her new contact at the station.

"Have you guys found something?" Holden brushed treat crumbs from his shirt. Sam noticed he was wearing a regular T-shirt and jeans today, not his usual dark blue FBI suit. Did that mean he was feeling more comfortable around them, and if so, was that a good thing or a bad thing?

Sam filled him in on their visit to the café. Major hopped down and sniffed at the crumbs on the floor, then gave Holden a dirty look and trotted off into Sam's office, presumably to hide in the closet, which had become his new favorite napping spot.

"Unfortunately we didn't get very much either," Holden said.

The rest of them took their seats, Jo sitting on top of her desk, her feet swinging in front, Sam with his hip leaning against the back of Kevin's desk, and Wyatt pulling his chair around to the front of his desk and turning it to face them.

Holden continued. "We've done the research into serial killings going back five years, but we haven't found anyone who hasn't already been arrested. There are a few unsolved cases, but none involving shallow graves." Holden glanced at Jo, and Sam wondered what that was about.

"So our guy is still out there," Sam said.

"Yes, but we might have a lead on the meth lab front."

"Really? Thorne?" Sam's voice was hopeful.

Holden took a deep breath. "I don't know if it is Thorne, but we have an informant in upstate New York who's worked with a meth lab out of northern New Hampshire. That lab is still in operation, and we're trying to find out where it is. They move around a lot to minimize getting caught. If it's linked to the cabin, we don't know, but he says the leader is someone who has a big business in northern New Hampshire."

Sam wasn't sure how he felt about that. On the one hand he desperately wanted to catch Thorne and put him in jail. On the other, it was a little annoying that the FBI had an informant all this time who might have been able to help his case against Thorne. Why hadn't they done this before? If they had, Thorne might be in jail right now. Then again, that wouldn't help the girls in the shallow graves.

"That sounds like Thorn," Wyatt said.

Holden made a face. "It sounds like him, but a lot of people have big businesses up here. We don't want to get fixated on Thorne and miss out on any clues that lead to someone else."

"Agreed," Sam said. "No sense in getting too excited.

The informant's meth lab owner might not be Thorne. Could be some other business owner, maybe even one of Thorne's minions. The important thing is catching whoever killed those girls and whoever was running the meth lab, whether it's Thorne or someone else."

"If it's the same person, that would make it all a little easier," Jo said.

"Even if the informant does identify Thorne, we're going to need physical evidence linking him with that cabin," Holden said.

"Did your lab find any DNA evidence linking the cabin to the shallow graves?" Sam asked. "I mean, scraps of fabric common to the two locations or something like that? You have a pretty sophisticated operation up there."

"We do, and that's why it's a little disconcerting that there was no evidence found linking them. It could be that the two are not related."

"Yeah, but was there any evidence at either spot that links to Thorne? A hair follicle, a drop of blood, anything?" Jo asked.

"Well, that's the problem. We don't actually have Thorne's DNA in the database," Holden said. "So the problem is we have to arrest him first with physical evidence that links him and then get his DNA so we can match it up."

"You mean Thorne's never been arrested?" Damn it! Thorne had been a juvenile when the case Mick had told him about had taken place. Those records were sealed, but they likely wouldn't have taken a DNA sample back then. Thorne had killed an animal, not a person, and back then they didn't have the technology for DNA sampling and preservation procedures that they did now.

"So what are you going to do next?" Sam asked.

Holden held up his hands. "Don't know. We're reaching somewhat of a dead end. The parents of the two victims who were identified couldn't help at all. The third one still hasn't been identified. We pulled out all the open missing persons cases. She doesn't match any of them."

Jo frowned. "How can that be?"

Holden's jaw tightened. "Unfortunately, there're a lot of people who just go missing and no one cares. Could be her parents were drug addicts. Could be her parents were dead and she was in the foster care system. Could be a lot of reasons."

Sam thought again about his daughters. He couldn't imagine not caring about what happened to them. Were there really parents so cold and unfeeling? He noticed Jo glance at her phone again, probably wondering if her sister might suffer a similar fate.

"One thing we could do is put surveillance on the café," Sam suggested. "It's a long shot, but if the killer is starting up again as the last email indicates, maybe he'll return to the café to email Menda again. If not a person, then maybe we could set up a camera outside the café. Those internet computers are right in the window. Then we could see who was at the computer at the time the email was sent."

Holden thought for a few seconds. "I'll see what I can do. I don't think we can allocate any manpower for it. We're stretched thin as it is, but maybe some kind of camera set up on the other side of the street might work. I'd need a warrant. I have to go back to head-quarters anyway. I'll let you know if anything new comes up."

"Thanks. I'll do the same," Sam said.

Wyatt spun his chair back behind his desk. "I'm going to dig into these emails a bit more. Maybe I can find something else."

"I'll search the newspapers to see if I can piece together an itinerary of Thorne's activities five years ago when the girls were murdered." Jo opened her laptop and started typing. "There might be articles about what he was building, which could give us some kind of a timeline. Maybe something will come up and we'll get lucky."

"I'm going to take another look through those crime scene photos." Sam headed to his office, Lucy trotting along beside him. He leaned his butt against the edge of the desk while he stared at the photos. Lucy sat beside him, her head tilted to stare up at the photos also, as if contemplating the evidence. He reached down to rub the fur on the top of her head. "There's got to be something in this physical evidence. It always comes down to a clue at the crime scene that we've overlooked."

He focused on the photos from the shallow graves, letting each one sift through his brain, tarps, holes, leaves, bones, scraps of clothing. The last body hadn't been identified. Should they focus on that? The thought haunted him that there was a family out there somewhere with a loving member who had never returned home.

Movement beside him stole his attention from the photos. Major had jumped up on his desk and sat beside him, staring solemnly at the cork board.

"Hi, there." Sam reached out tentatively to pet the cat. His fur was much softer than Lucy's. He glanced from the cork board to Sam, the contrast of his sleek jet black fur highlighting his luminescent golden eyes.

Lucy snorted, her eyes narrowing on the cat. She didn't make a move. She just watched him carefully.

Maybe she was getting used to Major. Better not pay too much attention to him, though. Lucy was still his favorite, and he wanted her to know that.

Sam turned back to the photos. The tarp. Thorne should have had some of those on the job site. Sam had never seen a construction site without tarps, but why didn't he have them? He must have known they were coming to inspect the site. Someone had tipped him off. Jamison? Freeman? Beryl?

The fact that the tarps were missing made Sam suspicious. He stared at the tattered blue scraps in the photos of the shallow graves. Those holes were so unusual. Tarps often had grommets, though not quite as many as these holes would indicate. Hadn't he read about a case in which a particular style of grommet had helped link physical evidence that solved the case?

But where were the grommets? It looked as though they'd either been ripped out or had fallen out. Perhaps the tarps had rotted around them and the grommets were still in the dirt. Maybe he should consider having someone take a metal detector up there and recover them. But there were too many holes. There wouldn't be that many grommets in the tarp. What were the other holes for?

Something clicked into place in Sam's mind. Thorne had been doing landscaping at the strip mall they passed on the way back from the café. Thorne had fought the improvement, but Mayor Dupont had stood firm on that one, at least.

The people of the town absolutely refused to have that mall built unless it had a certain amount of greenery. Sam wasn't surprised that Thorne had taken the cheap route and planted grass seed instead of springing for new sod. That old ground was hard with years of use and wouldn't grow nice lush grass without some work to get the water deep down to the roots.

That was where the aeration machine came in, and the aeration machine made dozens of tiny holes in the ground. Sam's gaze swiveled to the photos of the shallow graves again. The holes in the tarp, the mismatched pattern where there was one missing hole. Thorne's cheapness might be his downfall if his aeration machine had the same pattern and the distance between spikes matched the distance of the holes. This could be the break he'd been hoping for.

CHAPTER TWENTY-NINE

The landscape work was still in full swing when Sam and Jo got to the strip mall. They had taken Lucy, but not Wyatt. A call had come in that Bullwinkle was holding up traffic at the intersection of Hill and Maple, and Wyatt had volunteered to take care of the wayward moose while Sam and Jo headed out to look at the aerator.

Sam wasn't surprised that Thorne wasn't there. He liked to lord over his empire from his climate-controlled trailer. All the better, as Sam would get more cooperation from the workers who had stopped working and were now frowning at the Tahoe with its police insignia as it pulled in beside their trucks.

One guy, the largest of the three, had been running the aerator. He watched Sam and Jo approach. The other two went back to wrangling a four-foot-tall rhododendron into a hole, casting looks back at them every few seconds. Lucy busied herself sniffing each plant one by one.

The smell of bark mulch permeated the air, and the sun warmed Sam's back as he picked his way toward the guy, careful not to disturb the mulch or squash a plant. Sam's eye was drawn to the machine. This one was a rolling aerator and looked like a walk-behind lawn mower, except instead of cutting grass it propelled spikes down into the earth. It was the type that could make the holes Sam had seen in the tarps. He couldn't see the spikes from where he stood, but he hoped they'd match the diameter and spacing of those holes.

"Something wrong, officer?" The man asked.

"No." Sam gestured toward the machine. "Just wanted to get a good look."

"You need your lawn aerated?"

Sam laughed. Most times it paid to be friends. As his grandmother always said, you catch more flies with honey than vinegar. "Nah, just looking for something. Mind if I take a look?"

The man stepped aside. "Not at all."

Sam crouched down next to the machine, Jo beside him.

Sam glanced up at the man. "This job is for Thorne Construction, isn't it?"

The man nodded.

"So this equipment belongs to you or him?" Jo asked as Sam tipped the aerator on its side. The spikes were about two and a half inches long and a little thicker than a pencil. Did that match the size of the holes in the tarp? With the way the tarp had been frayed and ripped, it was hard to tell. But they seemed about the right size to Sam. Bev's lab had made a plaster mold of the holes from the piece of clay they'd dug out. They could easily prove it matched through that.

"Belongs to the company. We work for Thorne Construction." The man crouched beside them. "Is something wrong with it? I don't know anything about permits or specs. We just do what the company tells us."

"Nah, just wanted to get a look at it." Sam compared the spikes on the machine to what he remembered seeing at the grave site. The spikes seemed to be a bit farther apart. He'd have to call in for someone to measure them to be sure. He turned the cylinder slowly, studying each row of spikes, his hopes waning as he did.

There were no missing spikes. Whatever had made those holes in tarps in the graves wasn't this.

Jo looked at him over the top of her sunglasses, her gray eyes mirroring his disappointment. Another dead end.

Sam nodded. He put the machine right, dusted off his hands, and stood. "Is this the only aerator you have?"

The man nodded. "We only have the one. It usually does the trick."

"And when it doesn't?" Jo asked.

"We borrow one from another company."

"What's the name of that company?" Sam asked.

"Mervale International."

"SOMEHOW I DON'T THINK that getting a look at the Mervale landscaping equipment is going to be as easy as just walking up to the crew and turning a machine on its side," Jo said once they were back in the Tahoe.

"Think we need a warrant?" Sam asked.

"Unless you think Beryl Thorne will be nice enough to just show us whatever we want."

"She might, but if she isn't that might tip her or

Thorne off, and they could hide or destroy evidence before we get a chance to look," Sam said. "Better get a warrant."

The police radio under the dash squawked with a blast of static. "Let's make use of this thing."

Sam keyed the mic, "Reese, you there?"

Static and then, "Yes, chief, 10-4."

Sam glanced at Jo. "Um, can you fill out a search warrant form?"

"10-21."

"Huh?"

"You're not supposed to ask questions over the police radio, chief. You'll have to 10-21 that."

"What?"

"Call me on the phone." Reese sounded exasperated.

Sam rolled his eyes. "I finally find a use for this thing and I'm not supposed to use it for that?"

"Sorry, chief. Police protocol. People can listen in, you know."

Sam hadn't thought about that. Guess Reese had a point. "Okay, talk later."

"That's 10-4, chief."

Sam hung the mike up. "See? That thing is not useful, just like I said all along."

"I'll call her. Maybe we should talk to Jamison again and have him push it through," Jo said.

Jo pulled out her phone, ignoring the fact that there was no text from Bridget. She couldn't let that steal her attention away from the case right now. She needed to focus. She called Reese and relayed the information they needed on the form and then told her to fax it to Jamison.

Reese was quick, and the form was on Dottie's desk by the time Jo and Sam got there. Dottie had already arranged an audience with Jamison, who seemed a bit perturbed to find them in his office again.

"I just pushed a warrant through for you and it came back to bite me." Jamison smoothed his blue patterned tie. "And you didn't find anything?"

"He might have been tipped off," Sam said.

Jo watched Jamison's reaction. If he was the one who had tipped Thorne, she couldn't tell by the way he reacted.

"Judge Freeman will never agree to another warrant against Thorne. Thorne complained loudly about the last one. He made noises about a harassment lawsuit." Jamison said.

"This one isn't against Thorne," Sam said. "It's for Mervale International and it's solid. We're looking for a machine that can make a series of small holes like those found at the graves. The graves were linked to the cabin and Mervale is also linked to the cabin."

Jamison was silent. His eyes moved from Sam to Jo and then back again. Finally, he sighed and leaned back in his chair. "Fine. Judge Moseley is in today. I'll give him a call."

"Thank you." Sam started toward the door.

"Better hope this one isn't a bust," Jamison yelled after him.

Jo was skeptical about Jamison's motives in helping. He'd never seemed helpful before. Then again, he'd been in the shadow of Dupont. Had she misjudged him? But even if he did help, she was also skeptical about Moseley signing the warrant. They probably had a black mark against them from the previous one. But whatever Jamison had told him must have worked because the warrant was coming off the fax machine when Sam and Jo got back to the station. They grabbed it, did a quick about face, and headed right back out to Mervale.

CHAPTER THIRTY

Sam went straight to the back of the Mervale International parking lot, slowing as he passed the row of tall Lombardy poplars.

"I remember seeing some storage sheds back here when we came before." In the spaces between the trees, Sam saw the sheds. They were a little bigger than a residential tool shed, but looked a heck of a lot sturdier.

"I guess that's where they keep their equipment." Jo tapped the search warrant against her leg. "Let's go serve this and see what's inside."

The same blonde was behind the reception desk. Her eyes narrowed when she recognized them. "Are you here to see Mrs. Thorne?"

"No. This time we'd like to talk to the head of

maintenance." At least Sam hoped there was a head of maintenance. Someone had to manage the equipment, and a building this size would need someone to perform maintenance work on the facility.

"That would be Mr. Blakely. I'll see if he's in." She made the call, and Sam and Jo shuffled around the lobby for a few minutes until a tall, beefy guy in his mid-30s wearing a corporate emblem T-shirt and cargo pants appeared.

"I'm Jimmy Blakely." The man extended a calloused hand.

"Chief Mason. This is Sergeant Jody Harris."

They all shook, and the man shifted on his feet. "Is there something wrong?"

"We'd like to take a look at your landscaping equipment."

The man hesitated. "I don't know. What exactly is this about?"

Jo handed him the warrant. "Ongoing case. We're not at liberty to talk about it, but as you can see, we officially have the right to look."

"Oh." He looked down at the paper, and Sam could see he was torn over whether he should call his boss or simply lead them to the sheds. It didn't really matter much to Sam. The search warrant would get them in eventually. But they could get a look at the machine quicker if Jimmy didn't involve upper management. Sam hoped he wouldn't, because he was pretty anxious to find the machine that had made those holes so he could start moving on the case before Thorne did something drastic.

"Okay, this way." Jimmy walked to the door, and they followed. Sam's pulse picked up a notch. They were getting very close to a big break. "We keep it all out back in the storage sheds."

At the sheds, Jimmy pulled out a large ring of jangling keys and unlocked the doors.

"Do you have a lawn aerator?" Sam asked.

"Yeah. It's in that shed." Jimmy gestured toward the first shed. "It's in the back. Let me get this other stuff out."

Sam helped him pull out rakes, saw horses, and even one of those heavy-duty riding lawn mowers that commercial landscapers stood on to mow large lawns.

Finally, Jimmy pulled out the aerator. This one was a little different than the one they'd looked at earlier. It was narrower and looked heavier. Sam tipped it on its side, his hopes plummeting. Instead of the thin spikes, this one had round cylinders. Sam recognized them from some work he'd had done on one of the fancy Victorian homes one of his ex-wives had talked him into buying. The cylinders removed plugs of earth, churning them up and leaving them in the grass like Canada goose droppings. Unfortunately, the plugs were about a half-inch in diameter and three inches in between. They were too big and not spaced properly to be the machine that made the holes in the tarp.

"Is this the only aerator you have?" Sam asked.

"Yeah. We don't need more than one. Hardly use it," Jimmy said.

Jo glanced down at the machine. "What's wrong?"

"Wrong kind." Sam chewed his bottom lip. "But you probably had a different aerator before, right? Is this one new?"

"Nope. Look at the thing." Jimmy gestured to the mud-caked, rusted machine. "I've been here almost 10 years now, and this is the only one we've ever had. It still works okay, but like I said, we hardly ever use it."

"What's going on?" Beryl Thorne appeared between two poplars with a confused look on her face. "Chief Mason? What is this about?"

"We got a lead that links to some landscaping equipment."

"One that involves us? I thought you said nothing involves Mervale?"

"I didn't say our lead involved Mervale."

Beryl made a face. "And yet you're here."

Jimmy cut in, "I'm sorry, Mrs. Thorne. They had a warrant, and I thought I'd better comply. I hope it's okay."

"You did the right thing, Jimmy. Thanks. I'll take it from here." She held out her hand for the keyring. "I'll lock up when we're done."

Jimmy nodded, handed her the keys, and left. Then Beryl turned to Sam. "Just what is going on? If this is about that cabin, I thought it was clear that we didn't even own that place at the time in question."

"Right. Like I said, it's not Mervale that we have questions about."

Beryl crossed her arms over her chest. "Then why are you looking at our equipment?"

"The guy doing landscaping for Thorne Construction said that sometimes they borrow equipment from you."

Beryl's eyes narrowed. Fear? Suspicion? Or deviousness? "Thorne Construction? Yes, sometimes we lend them equipment. I mean, we do know each other. Is it Thorne Construction that's under suspicion?"

Sam made a noncommittal gesture, noticing how Jo was watching Beryl carefully for any signs that she had suspicions about her husband.

"Is this related to the reason you were at the café? Something about those emails?" Beryl asked.

"I can't really give out too much information." Sam glanced back at the aerator. Damn it. His one lead, and now it was a dead end. Then again, maybe Mervale wasn't the only place Thorne's landscaping crew borrowed equipment from. The Thornes themselves had quite a big estate, with a huge lawn to take care of. "Does Thorne Construction ever use landscaping equipment from your home?"

Beryl's eyes widened. "Our home? No. Just what are you insinuating?"

Sam held his hands up in a placating gesture. "I'm just following a lead. We think a piece of equipment is related to the skeletal remains."

"And you think that equipment might be at my home?" Her eyes darted from Sam to Jo. Sam almost felt sorry for her. After all, the poor thing *was* married to Lucas Thorne. And if getting her riled up served to have her give evidence against him later, it would be better for everyone, including her. Even if Thorne wasn't the killer, he was a drug dealer, and Beryl would be better off without him. "You're barking up the wrong tree. We don't have any landscaping equipment like this. We use a service."

Damn! It looked as though this really was a dead end.

"Okay, then. I'll put all this stuff back in the shed

for you." Sam rolled the aerator in, and Jo grabbed the wheelbarrow. Beryl picked up some rakes and followed them inside.

"I would like to know exactly what is going on. This is getting close to home, and I have a right to know if it concerns me," Beryl demanded.

Sam slid the aerator into place and looked at her. "I can't really say much as it's an ongoing case, but I think it is getting close to home for you. If you know anything, or have any suspicions, you should tell us."

"What do you mean? I don't know anything. How could I know something when I don't even know what you're talking about?"

Sam didn't have to be an expert in human behavior to tell by the way Beryl's eyes shifted to the left that she did know something. Now if he could only get her to say what it was. He contemplated telling her that Thorne had mutilated cats when he was younger. He figured that wouldn't sit well with an animal lover like her. But getting a wife to turn on her husband was a delicate balancing act. Sometimes they could become more defensive of their spouses. He needed to bring her along slowly and get her to come to her own real-ization that it was in her best interest to give them whatever she knew about Thorne.

Beryl sighed. "If I knew more about what your

suspicions were I might remember something or know what to look for."

Fishing for information? Was that because she was trying to make sure her husband really was into criminal activity? Or so that she could warn him?

"Let's just say there is compelling evidence that what went on at the cabin might link to something at Thorne Construction," Sam said.

Beryl blew out a breath, her eyes hardening as if she'd reached some sort of conclusion. Sam hoped that conclusion was that she should turn on her husband. She reached into her pocket, pulled out a card, and handed it to him. "My cell phone number is on here. I understand that you can't tell me specifics, but I'd appreciate a call if you discover that there's more you can tell me."

Sam accepted the card and put it in his pocket. Beryl turned to leave, then said, "It might be in your best interest to keep me informed because if I knew more I might know how I could help with the case."

CHAPTER THIRTY-ONE

B ack at the station, Lucy and Major must have sensed Sam's mood. There was no growling or hissing when Lucy tried to pass Major at his usual post atop the filing cabinet to greet Jo and Sam.

Wyatt looked up from his desk when they entered the squad room. "How did it go?"

"Dead end." Sam put his keys on the hook on the wall and went to the coffee machine. "Anyone want a coffee?"

"I'm good," Jo said, walking to her desk with the doughnut bag she'd snagged from Reese as they passed the dispatcher.

"Me too. But I have something that might help." Wyatt approached Sam with papers in his hand.

"When Reese said you were looking at the aerators, I did some research. I got the specs from the machines and measured the holes in the photos to compare them." Wyatt pointed to the columns on the paper. "Now, my numbers might be off because I was going by the photograph, and it's not life size. I have a call into the county lab to see if I can get the exact measurement from that chunk of clay we dug out at the site. This was just something quick I worked up so we could have something to work with right now."

The paper was neatly done. The hole sizes and spacing on the tarp were at the top, rows of measurements for the specs of the various machines under them. Sam didn't like what he saw. "None of these match the holes."

Wyatt nodded. I know. "But like I said, the math could be off."

"I don't know if it really matters. We're out of machines to look at," Sam said.

"Maybe we should go back to the drawing board with the holes." Jo pulled a toasted coconut doughnut from the bag.

"Did you get any more on those emails?" Sam asked Wyatt.

Wyatt shook his head.

"Maybe Holden Joyce got that surveillance set up," Jo said. "If what Menda said was true, our guy might be gearing up to send an email boasting about his intentions."

"Hopefully he'll do that before he actually kills someone else," Sam said.

Major jumped off the filing cabinet, landing with a soft thud. He hopped onto Jo's desk, peering into the bag.

"Do cats eat doughnuts?" Jo mumbled with her mouth full.

Major stuck his face in farther, his whole head disappearing into the bag.

"Guess so," Sam said.

Major shook off the bag, then hopped down, tell-tale crumbs in his whiskers. Lucy trotted over and sniffed the bag, which had fallen to the floor. Major apparently hadn't left much, because she went back to her place in the sun after a few sniffs.

"What about Beryl Thorne? Do you think she knows something?" Sam turned to Jo. "Didn't you think she was acting a little weird?"

Jo chewed thoughtfully. "Yep. It seemed like she was. I got the impression she knows something and was deciding whether she should tell us."

"How could she not know what Thorne is up to?" Wyatt asked. "She's his wife."

"Maybe they have separate lives," Sam said.

"Or she's in on it," Jo suggested. "She could be acting like she's concerned because she's trying to get information. I mean, seriously, if your spouse was a killer or a drug dealer, don't you think you would know? And if you knew you wouldn't stick with them unless you were working with them."

Sam shrugged. "There have been plenty of cases in which spouses didn't know. And besides, Thorne is kind of a jerk. Maybe their marriage isn't that great and she doesn't pay much attention to what he does."

"Well then, that could work in our favor, because if their marriage isn't that great maybe she's looking for a way to get rid of him."

"To get rid of who?" Bev Hatch came around the post office boxes.

"Thorne," Jo said.

Bev grunted. "Who wouldn't want to get rid of him? Did you get something on him?"

"We thought we did, but it turned out to be a dead end." Sam told her about their unsuccessful quest to find the aerator that made the holes in the tarps.

Bev stared at the photos, her face about two inches from the cork board. "Maybe there's some other kind of equipment that makes these holes. Are you sure they're relevant?"

Sam had been one hundred percent sure earlier. Now, not so much. "I don't know, but it's one piece of evidence we can use to tie to something physical. If we can just find something that makes this pattern of holes. Did your people find anything like that in the cabin?"

"I don't think so. I'll double check. It would be great if they did, because we haven't come up with much. The DNA analysis and meth lab investigation have basically flat-lined. We need something new."

"And it's not a stretch of the imagination that Thorne would have a piece of equipment that could do something like this. He owns a construction company," Jo said.

"It doesn't have to be a lawn aerator, right?" Bev asked.

"I guess not. What other kind of equipment should we look for?"

"Nail gun?"

"But that doesn't create a pattern. We need something that has a pattern that we can use to match to these holes." Sam tilted his head and looked at the pattern in the tarp. "Unless it is something like a nail gun and the killer, for whatever weird reason, shot a pattern, missing one spot."

"Maybe he didn't miss a spot." Wyatt looked at the cork board over Sam's shoulder. "Maybe something was in the way when he was making the pattern."

"Something that a spike couldn't pierce," Bev added.

"Like what?" Jo asked.

"I don't know. Metal? What else can't a spike go through? And what does this have to do with the bodies?" Wyatt asked.

Bev started pacing the room. "What if it has nothing to do with the bodies? Maybe the killer already had the tarp. It could be one Thorne had on his construction site. Maybe it was no good anymore because of the holes, and he decided to use it to wrap the bodies?"

"Even better," Jo said. "If he frequently uses whatever it is that makes the holes, that's a link we can tie back to him."

"If we can find whatever makes the holes," Bev said.

Sam studied Bev. "So, you really think it is Thorne too, then?"

Bev raised her brow. "I didn't say that. I'm just riffing off of what you said, but I wouldn't be disappointed if it was him, and we don't have any better leads."

"What about the FBI?" Wyatt asked. "They said they had some kind of informant. Maybe we can get to Thorne that way."

"Sure. Maybe that might get him some jail time for the meth lab. But if we could get him for this"——Sam tapped a photo of the shallow graves——"we could put him away forever. If only we had something better." Sam glanced at Jo, but Jo gave a subtle shake of her head. She hadn't heard from Bridget.

"Maybe we can put our heads together and think of another piece of equipment that might do this." Bev stopped her pacing and turned to stare at the board, her arms folded across her chest. "Or maybe we're wasting our time trying to pin this on Thorne."

"Hey. Anybody home?" Harry Woolston's voice bellowed from the lobby, accompanied by the annoying sound of metal scraping on marble.

Any other time, Sam would've gotten a kick out of Harry's outfit. He wore a plaid cap with a pom-pom on top, a white polo shirt, and what looked like knickers.

Jo screwed up her face. "What's with your outfit, Woolston?"

Harry made a face. "That's the wife. She's got me into all kinds of hobbies to keep me away from policing." Harry looked down at himself. "Now it's golf."

Lucy looked at him and whined.

"Don't worry. It's just me." Harry started toward the dog, his shoes scraping on the wide pine floors of the bullpen.

Sam winced. "Hey, would you mind taking those things off? You'll scratch up the floor with those cleats."

Harry lifted his foot. "What? These?"

Sam's eyes fell to the bottom of the shoe. Like Harry's outfit, they were old-school, with metal spikes. His eyes flicked from the bottom of the shoe to the photo of the holes in the tarp. "Harry, give me that shoe. I think you might've just provided a break in the case."

JO PEERED over Bev's shoulder as Sam pushed Harry into a chair, took his shoe, and then compared it to the holes in the photo. The photos weren't to scale, but it looked as though they could match. But then she'd thought that about the spikes in the aerator, too. She cautioned herself not to get her hopes up.

"Would golf cleats be able to puncture holes in a tarp?" Wyatt asked. "Those things are pretty tough."

"Probably not the new plastic ones, but these old metal spikes could," Sam said.

"But why would the killer wear golf shoes?" Bev asked.

"Who can say? He's not normal. We can't speculate on why he would do anything." Jo knew from her research that serial killers often had fetishes in which they exhibited odd behavior based on what had happened to them as children. She had no idea what this golf shoe fetish would be. Maybe his father was a golfer or he was abused by an uncle who golfed.

"But five years ago they had plastic ones, not these metal ones," Wyatt pointed out.

"Sure, but the metal ones can still be purchased, right Harry?" Jo asked.

"Yeah, the missus got these over at the secondhand store." Harry wiggled his toes, now clad only in a sock.

"We don't even know if Thorne golfs," Bev said.

Sam turned to face her. "Actually we do. I saw a golf trophy when I was in his construction trailer the other day."

"We need to get a warrant," Jo said. "Then we need to get that casting your lab made of the holes in the clay, Bev."

"No problem on the casting. But good luck with the warrant. I heard Judge Freeman was already upset about the last one," Bev said.

"Yeah, Thorne has him in his pocket, but maybe we won't need a warrant." Sam held a business card up, and Jo recognized it as the one Beryl Thorne had given them. "Maybe we can convince the evidence to come to us."

Sam disappeared into his office, and Jo headed out to the lobby. Even though Reese had gone home, Jo knew where she kept the forms used to request warrants. She figured Sam was calling Beryl, but she had her doubts about whether or not Beryl Thorne was going to turn her husband in.

Sitting at the reception desk, she glanced at her phone for the umpteenth time. Still no message from Bridget.

Now she was starting to wonder if this did have anything to do with Thorne. The irrigation machines had been a big failure. What if this golf thing was, too?

She busied herself filling out the form while Wyatt and Bev took measurements from Harry's shoes, much to his delight. Judging by the conversation filtering in from the squad room, Harry was happy to be part of the investigation, even if it didn't entail going out in the field. At least this was something his wife wouldn't protest about too much.

Just when Jo had finished filling out the form, the door opened. In came Beryl Thorne, holding a paper bag out in front of her, as if it contained a smoking gun, which, if it was the golf shoes, it very likely did. Her eyes darted around the room quickly. "Is Chief Mason in?"

CHAPTER THIRTY-TWO

Sam came out of his office to find Beryl Thorne standing in the squad room holding a bag. So, she had come after all. When he'd gotten off the phone with her, he hadn't been sure she would. She had sounded incredibly uncertain.

He rushed over to her and took the bag. "Thank you so much for coming."

She looked as if she might bolt at any minute, her eyes flicking from Sam to the bag. "I brought his golf shoes like you asked." Her voice was shaky.

Sam put a reassuring hand on her shoulder. "You did the right thing. This is important."

She swallowed hard and nodded.

Sam opened the bag. Inside was an old pair of golf shoes, similar to the ones Harry was wearing. They had metal cleats crusted with dirt. Apparently, Thorne didn't take very good care of his shoes. Either that, or because he had used them while burying the victims he didn't want them cleaned off. Some kind of weird serial killer souvenir, perhaps? All the better for Sam. Maybe that dirt would contain evidence they could use against him.

"You won't tell him I gave you these, will you?" Beryl asked.

Sam glanced up from the bag. Beryl looked frightened. "No, of course not." At least Sam hoped they wouldn't have to, but if they did it would be during Thorne's trial, and he'd be locked away, unable to retaliate against his wife.

Beryl wrapped her arms around herself, her eyes glued to the bag. "I suspected Lucas hadn't been right for a while, but I never imagined he could be involved in something this horrible."

Sam had already put on gloves and was lifting the shoes out of the bag to inspect them further. His heart leapt when he noticed that one spike was missing.

Wyatt ripped the photo from the cork board and brought it over for comparison. It looked as if the pattern matched.

"Does it help?" Beryl stared at the photo, her voice trailing off.

"Yes. Thank you very much. It helps." Sam turned her around and walked her toward the lobby. He had important work to do, and it wouldn't help to have the wife of the man he was about to arrest in the station. "How did you get these? Was your husband at home when you took them?" Sam hoped Thorne hadn't seen her taking the golf shoes. It might tip him off and cause him to run.

"He was at home, but out back in the tool shed. He didn't see me leave. He was busy rearranging his tools."

Or hiding more evidence, Sam thought.

"Maybe you should go to your parents or somewhere else other than home."

Her eyes registered alarm at his words. "Are you going to arrest him now?"

"Possibly. I'll let you know."

Beryl left, and Sam ran back to the squad room.

"I've already called Holden Joyce," Bev said. Then, at the obvious look of disappointment on Sam's face, she added, "I know he's a pain, but he can expedite a search warrant for Thorne's place. You guys seem to have a hard time pulling that off, you have to admit."

She had a point. "What did he say?"

"He's on it. He'll get a warrant as fast as he can and let us know."

"Great." Sam grabbed his keys from the hook on the wall.

"Aren't you going to wait for—?"

Sam interrupted Bev's question. "No time for that. We might be able to catch him in the act of destroying evidence, but if we wait too long there might not be anything left. He didn't have any tarps or hoses or duct tape at his construction site, but he might have them stored at home. His wife said he was in his tool shed. We don't have time to wait." Sam glanced at Harry, but the ex-chief was already holding his palms up in front of him.

"I'll sit this one out, Sam."

"Good thinking. You broke the case. That's enough for one day."

Sam pointed to Lucy, who stood at attention next to Harry. "Come on, girl. This time you can come."

Bev and Wyatt were already in the lobby, with Jo close behind. Sam jogged to catch up, yelling over his shoulder to Harry, "Don't wait up, and try not to piss off the cat."

THORNE LIVED in a small mansion in the affluent section of town. They drove down streets lined with stately oaks, the properties spaced several acres apart. Thorne's house was a three story-brick manse with lush landscaping. It was dark now, but Sam could still see that the lawn was meticulously groomed and every hedge perfectly trimmed.

The house was dark. He hoped Beryl had taken his advice and gone elsewhere. He didn't want her to get hurt if things went squirrely.

Sam saw a shaft of light spilling from the door of a shed through the break in the hedges that separated the front yard from the back. The faint smell of wood smoke drifted toward him, and his gut clenched. Was Thorne burning the evidence?

He started toward the shed, but Bev grabbed his arm. She leaned over and whispered, "Holden texted. He's on the way. They'll be here in twenty minutes."

Sam's gaze didn't waver from the shed. There was a large window on one side, and a shadow moved back and forth. Thorne was busy in there, and Sam wasn't going to wait for the FBI.

"Good. Then they should get here for the good stuff. Follow me, but stay behind."

Sam squeezed through the hedge, sticking to the shadows. He didn't want to take a chance that Thorne might spot him and bolt. Beside him, Lucy quietly sniffed the air. When he rounded the corner of the house he saw the golden flames of a bonfire flickering in the fire pit. He hoped the evidence they needed against Thorne wasn't going up in flames.

Sam didn't want to spook Thorne, so he motioned for the others to hold back as he slowly approached the door. Inside, Thorne was loading a metal wheelbarrow that sat in the middle of the shed. Sam craned his neck to see what was inside, but he couldn't quite make it out from where he stood.

He moved forward, and Thorne spun around, squinting out into the night. His eyes widened as he recognized Sam.

"Mason, what the hell are you doing here? This is private property."

"Just out walking my dog." Sam stepped closer. Now he could see inside the wheelbarrow——rubber hosing and a few half rolls of duct tape.

Thorne scowled and pulled a phone from his pocket. "This time you've gone too far. I'm calling Jamison. I'll have you arrested for trespassing."

"Who's going to arrest me?"

"The county sheriff."

"I don't think so. She's here with me. And the FBI is on the way."

Thorne looked doubtful, but his finger hovered over the phone. "You're bluffing."

"Give it up, Thorne. We have a search warrant and evidence that proves you're the meth distributer and serial killer we've been looking for." At least, Sam hoped they had a search warrant. If Holden was on his way, he must've gotten one.

"What are you talking about?" Thorne's voice rose.

"What have you got in the wheelbarrow? Maybe some tarps or souvenirs from your kills?"

"You've got the wrong guy, I haven't killed anyone."

Sam took a closer look. No tarps, but he didn't let that get him down. They had plenty with the hoses and duct tape, and given the fact that Thorne was clearly trying to do something with them, he felt certain they could be linked to the meth lab. "I see you've got some items one might find in a meth lab. In fact, we found some stuff just like this in an old meth lab recently."

He was inside the shed now, his eyes scanning for the brilliant blue of a tarp. Nothing. Where had he hidden them? The wood smoke wafted in. The fire! Had he already burned them?

Sam hollered over his shoulder, "Bev, Jo, douse that fire. There could be something in there."

Thorne scowled. "It's just a bonfire, Mason. I don't know what you're talking about. This stuff is just duct tape, common gardening stuff." Thorne stepped around the wheelbarrow. "You can't just come in here and accuse me."

Sam's hand hovered over his gun. Thorne was not armed, but the shed was full of tools he could use as a weapon.

Next to him Lucy growled, and Thorne's eyes flicked to the dog. The hair on the back of her neck stood up. He took a step backward. "This is harassment."

"Not when you're actually a criminal, it isn't," Sam pointed out.

"Why do you keep saying that?" Thorne demanded. Sam had to hand it to him. He was denying it till the end.

The sound of sirens split the air. Bev must've found something in the fire and relayed that information to Holden Joyce. Otherwise they would've come in silently.

Thorne's eyes took on a wild look. He was coming unglued. "You'd better back off, Mason," he hissed. "Don't forget, I have something on you and your buddy."

Of course Thorne would bring that up, but just

what did he actually have? The knife itself didn't really prove much. Or did it? Had Thorne and Dupont somehow done something to add DNA evidence incriminating Sam and Mick of something they hadn't done? All the better to see Thorne in jail tonight, where he couldn't use it against him. Was the knife hidden here in his shed? In his office? They'd be searching both, and Sam made a mental note to have an active hand in those searches. "Sorry, Thorne. I'm not afraid of you or your threats."

"This is preposterous! You don't have anything on me!" But the trapped look in his eyes as he glanced at the wheelbarrow told Sam that they did indeed have something.

"You can cut the innocent act. We know you were in contact with Menda and sent emails from the café."

Thorne's brows mashed together as if he were starting to believe his own lies. "Café? Emails? What are you talking about?"

The silence grew louder, and Thorne became more agitated.

"How long are you going to play dumb? It's over, Thorne. We have your golf shoes."

"Golf shoes? I haven't golfed in decades." Thorne's eyes narrowed, darting from the window to Sam. "Where did you get my golf shoes anyway?"

"I told you, we have a warrant." Sam was purposely vague. He didn't want to get Beryl into trouble, just in case the charges against Thorne didn't stick. "And what's with the bonfire outside? I bet we'll find that you're burning evidence."

Tires screeched in the driveway. Thorne glanced at the window again. Surely he wasn't thinking about...

Thorne took two steps back, then made a running dive toward the window. The glass shattered. Lucy gave one warning bark and took off around the shed.

When Sam got to the other side of the shed, Lucy was holding Thorne pinned to the ground about twenty feet from the window. He hadn't gotten very far. Holden Joyce and several FBI agents ran through the hedge.

"Let me go! I'm innocent!" Thorne thrashed, but Lucy held tight.

Holden glanced from the broken window to Thorne. "Right. Innocent guys usually jump through windows to get away."

Sam called Lucy off, and the FBI agents cuffed Thorne and began reading him his rights. Sam took Holden to the wheelbarrow to show him the evidence.

Wyatt, Jo, and Bev had managed to extinguish the fire and were pulling out melted scraps of duct tape.

"Bag it all up," Holden said. "The duct tape at the

cabin was made with a certain adhesive that was defective. It was used for only a few months. If this matches, it's one more thing we have against him."

"And your informant?" Sam asked.

Holden nodded. "Hopefully he'll come through. We're going to need that. The duct tape is circumstantial, but it adds up."

"We have the golf shoes back at the station. Forensics might be able to find blood under those cleats if we're lucky. Maybe epithelials on the inside that match to Thorne."

"Let's hope so," Holden said as they started back toward the FBI agents, who were now attempting to drag Thorne toward the car.

"I demand to know what this is about!" Thorne screamed.

"You've been read your rights. You're being arrested." Holden gestured toward the wheelbarrow, which was now outside surrounded by more FBI agents who were bagging the contents. "We have plenty of evidence showing you running a meth lab, and possibly enough to link you to a series of shallow graves."

Thorne bucked and tried to pull away from the agents. "I told you, I'm innocent."

"Sure you are," Holden said, "You'll get your day in court."

Sam stood beside Holden Joyce, watching them pull Thorne away. Thorne turned around, his face red with fury as he spit the words at Sam, "I'll get you back, Mason!"

"He's protesting an awful lot about this," Holden said.

Sam watched as they shoved Thorne in the car. "Won't take him long to learn that he can't wriggle out of this easily. With what we have, we should be able to prove Thorne was at least involved with the meth lab, and hopefully we'll find evidence on the golf shoes that will tie him to the killings. I'm not surprised he's protesting, though. That guy is so arrogant he probably thinks he can just claim he's innocent, pay off a judge, and get off."

Holden shook his head. "Considering he was caught destroying the evidence, I don't think that's going to happen. No judge in his right mind would take that payoff."

CHAPTER THIRTY-THREE

D im lighting created a hushed sense of twilight in the hospital room. The only sound was the constant beeping of the machines.

Sam leaned against the bedrail, looking down at the still body. "Well, we finally got Thorne."

Kevin didn't answer, didn't even twitch a muscle. Not that Sam expected him to. He hadn't shown any signs of knowing anyone else was there on Sam's previous visits, and Sam didn't think he would now. But someday he would. Even though the doctor had said he'd lost so much blood it had been very traumatic to his system and he may never recover, Sam knew he would.

Sam wondered if somewhere in there Kevin could hear him. Probably not. The trips he'd been making to update him were more for Sam's benefit than for Kevin's.

Sam started to pace alongside the bed, his steps keeping time with the constant beeping of the heart monitor. "We have solid evidence for the meth lab. The FBI was able to match some things found in the abandoned cabin with things Thorne had in his shed. We finally got a search warrant to look through his house and office. Remember how many times we tried to do that before?" Sam glanced at Kevin as if he would magically answer the question, but he just lay there. The machines continued to beep.

Sam turned and paced back up toward the head of the bed again. "Did I mention his wife was instrumental in helping us nail him?"

Sam paced back down to the foot of the bed. "Yeah, and forensics found blood under the cleats of the golf shoes she gave us, so we're well on our way for nailing him for being a serial killer, too." Sam stopped the pacing and turned around. He frowned at the pale officer in the bed. "Though some of the details on that seem a little sketchy."

He shrugged and continued the pacing. "And of course, Thorne denies it all, especially the serial killings, but who wouldn't? He could go away for a long time for those three girls. We're just hoping there weren't more."

Sam stopped at the head of the bed again, leaned on the railing, and looked down at Kevin. "Anyway, Harry still blames himself for what happened to you, so the sooner you wake up and ease his conscience, the better. He's no spring chicken, you know, and of course Lucy misses you."

A slight movement made Sam's heart leap. Was that an eye twitch? Sam leaned closer, staring at Kevin's eyes. He could have sworn he'd seen a little flutter when he'd mentioned Lucy.

"Kevin, can you hear me?"

Kevin didn't move. Had it been his imagination? He glanced at the machines. They were still beeping at the same rate. No alarms, no nurses running. Wouldn't they have some monitors on Kevin to know if he was waking up? Wouldn't someone come? He leaned in closer. "Kevin, buddy. Can you hear me? We need you back at the department."

But Kevin didn't move.

"Well, I just wanted to give you an update. The others are waiting at Holy Spirits to celebrate." Sam turned to leave, then looked back at Kevin. "I wish you could join us. Maybe next time?"

Sam caught a nurse in the hallway. "Is there any improvement with Officer Deckard?"

The nurse smiled and shook her head.

"I thought I saw his eyes twitch."

The nurse's smile turned sad. "I don't think so. He's in pretty deep. It's going to be a long haul for him. In fact, we're moving him to a long-term care facility now that he's stable."

Sam nodded. He knew Kevin's brother had signed the paperwork to move him into Longview, but Sam was still holding out hope that Kevin would wake up before then.

"Okay. Let me know if anything changes," Sam said.

"We will. Have a good night, chief."

"You too." Sam turned and left, ready to join the livelier crowd at Holy Spirits.

JO WAS ALREADY on her second beer when Sam slid onto the bar stool next to her at Holy Spirits. She had been anxious for him to show up because she had important news that might help solidify the case against Thorne.

"Sorry I'm late, I stopped to visit Kevin." Sam signaled Billie for a beer.

Jo glanced up from her own beer, hopeful. "Was there a change?"

Sam shook his head. "Nope. I just like to keep him updated. The nurse said they might be moving him soon."

Jo nodded. "Yeah, I heard his brother signed the paperwork and closed up Kevin's house for the winter. His badge and the stuff he got from the hospital is waiting for him in your closet. You know, when he comes back."

"Hopefully that'll be soon." Sam accepted his beer from Billie. "I don't know if he can hear me, but I was hoping the news about Thorne's arrest would sink in and bring him back to us."

"Speaking of which, I have something that might help us." Jo held the phone up, and Sam's eyes widened. "Your sister?"

Jo nodded. Bridget had finally replied to one of her texts, and much to Jo's delight, she was still working on cleaning up her act. "She's in a program. I broached the topic of her identifying the man she saw Amber with, but she seemed a little reluctant."

"Maybe we should give her some time," Sam suggested.

"Probably, but we may not have time. Isn't Thorne fighting this and still insisting he was framed?"

"Yeah, but I'm not too worried. We have evidence against him. I'm just glad your sister is okay."

Jo's heart warmed at the genuine look of concern on Sam's face. Guilt gnawed away the warmth of friendship. Now was the time to tell him about her other sister. Her gaze drifted over her shoulder to see Wyatt approaching. Darn! She didn't want to do that in front of Wyatt.

"Hey guys, this place is great!" Wyatt stood between Jo and Sam, looking up at the stained-glass window.

"You've never been here before?" Jo asked.

"Nope. I usually spend my time closer to home, but now that I work in White Rock, I guess this kind of is home."

"Nice job on the work you did on the Thorne case." Sam shook Wyatt's hand.

Wyatt blushed. "Hey, just doing my job."

Jo studied Wyatt. He was modest and a good cop. Yep, things were gonna work out between them just fine.

"I missed all the excitement, but I can still celebrate." Reese appeared, a white paper bag in her hand.

She passed the bag to Jo. "Brewed Awakening has jelly doughnuts again. I got you one."

Jo looked inside the bag and smiled. Then she closed it up. Doughnuts and beer? They really didn't go together that well. She'd save it for later. Still, the fact that her favorites were back was a good sign. Jelly doughnuts, her sister in a recovery program, and Thorne in jail. Things were looking up in a big way.

"Anyway, I got your text and just shot over to have a quick drink with you guys. I fed Lucy and Major, and they're snoozing away at the station." Jo had figured since she'd invited Wyatt she should invite Reese, too, so she'd texted her to see if she could join them.

Sam laughed. "Are you sure? There's no telling what the two of them could get up to with nobody there to referee."

"No, it seems things have calmed down between the two of them. At least Lucy let Major get within five feet of her food bowl tonight without growling."

"If you say so."

Reese ordered a shot of tequila and then turned back to Sam and Jo. "Bev Hatch stopped by the station. She said the last girl was identified. She was from Wyoming. She's hoping maybe the parents will know something further that we can use in the case."

"That would be good." Jo swigged her beer. It was almost empty.

Sam held his beer up in a greeting toward someone behind Jo's back. Judging by the scowl on Reese's face, Jo didn't need to turn around to see who it was.

"What is Marnie Wilson doing here?" Reese gave Sam a pointed look.

Sam took a swig. "Heck if I know. She's campaigning now, so she's probably trying to get the vote of the working people."

"You sure she didn't come to see you?" Reese didn't mince words.

Sam made a face. "Why would she come to see me?" As if to prove his words, he turned back to the bar, away from Marnie.

Reese looked toward the door. "Isn't that your friend Mick?"

Sam followed her gaze. "Yep."

"Come on, Wyatt. Let's go grab the table." Reese nodded toward a table that had just been vacated by a rowdy after-work crowd. "There isn't enough room for all of us at the bar."

Reese and Wyatt passed Mick on the way to the table. Mick slid in on the other side of Sam. Billie had the whiskey glass on the bar before Mick's butt hit the chair.

"So what are you gonna do now that your favorite bad guy is in jail?" Mick asked Sam.

Sam chuckled. "It'll be a welcome break not to have to tangle with him."

"Do you think the construction will stop?" Mick asked.

"I hope so. His wife is in charge now, and she seems a lot more environmentally friendly."

Jo picked the label on her beer. She certainly hoped so too. She hated the strip malls and hotels that were springing up around White Rock, but somehow she had a feeling that Beryl Thorne wasn't exactly as friendly as Sam thought she was. There was something about the woman that gave her pause, but she couldn't quite put her finger on exactly what it was.

Mick leaned in closer and lowered his voice. "And did you find the item of interest?"

Sam shook his head. "I was in on the searching of his home, his office, and the shed. I didn't find the knife."

Jo's gaze flicked from Sam to Mick. "He probably hid it somewhere. Is that really going to be an issue now that he's in jail?"

Sam's jaw tightened. "Hopefully not, but he might have left it with one of his minions. Maybe he'll try to use it as leverage to get a lighter sentence."

Mick tossed back his drink. "I guess we'll have to wait and see."

"Oh crap, is that Holden Joyce?" Sam squinted into the mirror at the crowd behind them, and Jo followed his gaze to see the FBI agent making his way toward them. "I thought he would just go away once this case was over."

"I'll let you guys talk shop." Mick picked up his drink and headed to join Reese and Wyatt at the table.

"Sam, Jo." Holden shook their hands. He seemed quite happy, jovial even. A big change from the original Holden Joyce they'd met on the last case. Apparently capturing a serial killing drug dealer was good for his spirits.

"How's our favorite criminal?" Sam asked. "Still denying everything?"

Holden blew out a breath. "Yep, but we're getting more and more evidence. We've linked more of the supplies in the cabin to him, and we're still working on an eyewitness."

"But what about the meth lab and the shallow graves? Is there anything more than that one leaf to link them?" Sam asked.

Jo knew that one leaf wouldn't be enough to prove that Thorne was involved in killing those girls. Even if they proved he was at the cabin, and they linked the cabin with the gravesites, it was all circumstantial. The golf shoes that Beryl Thorne had given them were going to be important evidence in the case.

Jo glanced down at her phone, then finished her beer. Holden didn't know about her sister yet, and she was going to keep it that way. She wasn't going to volunteer her sister's services until Bridget felt comfortable trying to identify Thorne. It was more important that her sister not have anything to stress over while she tried to get clean.

"He's screaming about a setup and suing the police department," Holden said. "What's a guy gotta do to get a beer around here?" He leaned over the bar.

Sam signaled for Billie, then tapped Holden on the shoulder and pointed toward the table where Reese, Wyatt, and Mick now sat. "We're over at that table when you get your beer."

"I'll be there in a second too." Jo held up her empty beer. "I need to order another one myself."

Holden slipped into Sam's chair and leaned over the bar to catch Billie's attention. "This one's on me," Holden said as they ordered the two beers.

Holden spun his seat to face her. The look on his face made her uncomfortable. Then again, the guy had been acting weird towards her the whole case. Why should now be any different?

"The evidence against Thorne isn't exactly conclusive, but I know he deserves to be in jail. That said, he's not the guy responsible for your sister."

Jo's heart knocked against her ribcage. Holden Joyce knew about her sister? Of course he did. That was why he'd been acting the way he had been. He'd probably known she'd also been conducting her own unauthorized investigation all these years.

Holden nodded. "Yes, I know about your sister. And I talked to O'Reilly, too. I know you have some expertise in serial killers."

"Have you been checking up on me? Why?" Jo was miffed. What was the FBI guy angling at? Even though he hadn't been such a pain in the ass on this case, she still didn't really want to be friends.

"When I was a rookie I had a serial killer case." Holden's eyes glazed over in a haze of painful memories. "We didn't catch the guy. Ten children were brutalized and killed. I vowed that I would get him. I think he might be the same guy who took your sister."

Jo felt it like a punch in the gut. At first she was suspicious. Surely Holden Joyce was up to something. This was too convenient. She did the math in her head. Holden was about ten years older than her. He would have been fresh out of the academy and a newbie FBI agent when her sister was taken.

She remembered the cases of the other children. Had Holden been searching for this killer his whole career, just as she had? No wonder he had been so diligent. He didn't want to mess up again. And if what he was saying was true, then someone else believed that her sister's abductor was still out there. She wasn't alone.

"The police never found any similar cases after Tammy was taken. They had always worked under the assumption that the man who took my sister was eventually caught and incarcerated for other crimes, and never admitted to taking her," Jo said.

"Is that what you believe?" Holden paid for the beers that Billie shoved across the bar and slid one to Jo.

Jo studied his face. She was good at reading people. Holden wasn't conning her. He was serious about catching this killer, and he valued her opinion. "No, I think the person is still out there."

Holden nodded. "I do too, but the guy who killed the women in these graves, it's not him. And Thorne couldn't have been the one who took your sister. He was in Europe backpacking during that time. He would have been very young."

"Yes, but as we both know, serial killers can start very young."

"My case and your sister's case are too old and too cold for the police to care about. But both of us seem to have a little bit of expertise in the subject. What do you say we combine forces and try to catch this guy?" Holden's face turned serious. "If he's still out there, he could kill again."

Jo took a sip of beer, then turned her chair to face the room. Reese, Sam, Wyatt, and Mick were laughing at the table. Her heart clenched when she watched Sam. It should be Sam she was teaming with to catch a serial killer, not Holden Joyce.

"So what are you suggesting? The killer would be quite old now."

"That doesn't stop them from killing," Holden said. "It wouldn't take much. We'd be doing the same thing that you've probably already been doing. The same thing that I've been doing—gathering information, investigating on the side. What do you think? Are you in?"

Jo slid her thumbnail under the beer label. Investigating her sister's case had consumed her, eaten up her whole life, and now that she was finally making a home here in White Rock she'd vowed to set it aside. But this new case had ripped the scabs off the old wounds, fueling the desire to investigate and find justice for her sister again.

"I'll have to think about it. Maybe."

Holden glanced toward the table. "Does Mason know about your sister?"

Jo sighed, "No." Why hadn't she told Sam? Looking back, it seemed she'd had a million chances, but something always came up. Was it because she'd always had an excuse not to tell him because she felt guilty about not being up front with him when she'd first come to town? Now she felt it was a huge betrayal of their friendship.

"You going to tell him?"

"Yes. Sam and I are partners. We don't keep secrets like that from each other."

Holden glanced at her. "Well, you've kept it so far."

"Yeah, but no more. I'm going to tell him just as soon as I find the right time."

She'd have to tell him if she was going to start this investigation on the side with Holden. Before she'd been on her own. It had been tough getting leads, getting people to talk to her. She didn't have access to police files or databases, but the help of an FBI agent would make things much easier. She was definitely going to take Holden Joyce up on his offer. After all, what did she have to lose?

****

JOIN my readers list to get notification about the next Sam Mason mystery:

http://ladobbs.com/newsletter

Books in the Sam Mason Series:

Telling Lies (Book 1)
Keeping Secrets (Book 2)
Exposing Truths (Book 3)
Betraying Trust (Book 4)

Did you know that I write mysteries under other names? Join the LDobbs reader group on Facebook on find out! It's a fun group where I give out inside scoops on my books and we talk about reading!

https://www.facebook.com/groups/ldobbsreaders

ALSO BY L. A. DOBBS

Sam Mason Mysteries

***

Rockford Security Systems (Romantic Suspense)

*Formerly published with same titles under my pen name Lee Anne Jones

ABOUT THE AUTHOR

L. A. Dobbs also writes light mysteries as USA Today Bestselling author Leighann Dobbs. Lee has had a passion for reading since she was old enough to hold a book, but she didn't put pen to paper until much later in life. After a twenty-year career as a software engineer, she realized you can't make a living reading books, so she tried her hand at writing them and discovered she had a passion for that, too! She lives in New Hampshire with her husband, Bruce, their trusty Chihuahua mix, Mojo, and beautiful rescue cat, Kitty.

Her book "Dead Wrong" won the "Best Mystery Romance" award at the 2014 Indie Romance Convention.

Her book "Ghostly Paws" was the 2015 Chanticleer Mystery & Mayhem First Place category winner in the Animal Mystery category.

Join her VIP Readers group on Facebook:
https://www.facebook.com/groups/ldobbsreaders

Find out about her L. A. Dobbs Mysteries at:
http://www.ladobbs.com

Made in United States
Orlando, FL
07 September 2023

36802879R00187